AF593686

FOR SWORD AND PLANET

Cover art by Ella Gillespie

First Edition

Dedicated to Aunt Steph, Uncle Paul, and Uncle Mike, for encouraging me to follow my craft.

PROLOGUE

The Rosewood Knight stared at the twilight forest, just as it stared back.

He inched his way down the mountainside, aided by no path, trail, or other such luxuries. At a close glance, the stone was a dull red and brown. Nothing of note, just gravel and pebbles that crumbled beneath the boot. However, as the setting sun illuminated the mountain in all its glory, the Rosewood Knight looked onwards and saw the shimmering red and orange and blue stripes of earth that made up the wild range. Even as the light glinted from his silver helm, lined with gold, he took no interest in the natural wonders. Gauntlets over his hands, he gripped them against the rock, taking great care not to tumble into the black that lay far, far below. A frigid breeze caught his cloak, sweeping the dark red fabric into wind, and further chilling his well-worn visor.

"VVitch lies near," muttered Rose's companion, Sir Brimeor. The knight wore a blue suit of armor tinged with green, its ancient metals cracked and emanating black light. His face was uncovered, exposing pale skin laden with a hard scowl, and a head of dark hair blowing in the wind. "Look to the dead trees in the valley below. Can you see a house that stands tall? Amongst the lich-ridden ground and whispering shadow?"

Their third companion momentarily lost her balance, scraping her suit against the rock until she caught a piece of the mountainside that jutted outwards, creating a flat enough perch. Lady Haera, or the Selkie, as she was colloquially known, brushed dirt off her vibrant green breastplate, sweeping a rune-inscribed cloak with her brown hands, so as not to get her legs tangled. She wore a helm of the same blinding color, though she, like Brimeor, kept her face visible. The Rosewood Knight was the only one who hid his face. "I see it not, Sirs, though I fear the shadow's thirst to serve VVitch only grows with nightfall. Mayhaps we should make camp, and descend on the morn."

Already, the sun had set behind the mountains on the far side of the valley. The multicolored rock was covered in shadow, accompanied by the tremendous vegetation that grew on the high terrain. Thick, beige stalks broke through the hard earth, widening into what resembled moss-covered boulders that spread themselves until they were dull green, shrub-like leaves. Rose estimated that if he were to stand on top of himself, he could just touch the top of the strange plants. They were rich and alive, unlike the forest below.

The Rosewood Knight shook his head. "Nay. It makes no matter the hour of our descent. The trees block all light, whether it be moon or solar. Shadows dance beneath, just as powerful under the cover of darkness as they are in the boiling day. Were we not to make haste, that would mean another day of rotting crops. Famine. Disease. As knights of the realm, it is our duty –"

By then all three of them stood on the same rock, resting their strained muscles. Haera spat at Rose's feet. "I come as an embassy for the Midnight Sea. You know this, Rosewood Knight, for you tried your best to keep me from joining you on this jest of an errand." *That, and many a reason more*, Rose thought to himself. She kept talking. "I know not from where Sir Brimeor hails, but I suspect you despise him just as me, or at least do not give him regard as you do others. Let us not keep this poor farce between us, shall we? Not when we approach imminent doom. I know the real reason you roam the Heartlands. It is not to rid it of evil, nor because of any notion of justice."

Brimeor huffed. "Sir Rose *asked* me to come with, as a proud warrior of the Evermeadow. He did not ask you. If you wish to tear down this self-perceived veil of idiocracy, then act the part of a knight and cease the air of jealousy and lies."

Lady Haera turned red and rounded on him. "There are sailors like you who roam the sea. Ones who share your superstitions. Were it not for the Codex, I would not hesitate to teach you the lesson you seem so desperate to learn." The Rosewood Knight laid a hand on her shoulder. She wacked it away, hissing: "Don't touch me."

"My friends," Rose spoke up. "Now is not the time to bicker amongst ourselves." They fell silent, Haera glowering, Brimeor smirking. Teeth poked out behind his smile, yellow and pointed. Rose continued: "Lady Haera, I will not deny that I hadn't wished for you to join us on this perilous quest, but you are here now, and any extra blade will do us no harm in the fight to come. Brimeor, you are my honored guest, and I trust you shall follow suit of your host and put aside your differences." He nodded. Haera looked ready to do him harm. "Embrace your sailor's spirit and throw your grievances into the murky waters. Lady Haera, I shall forgive you putting my honor into question. Words, they were, nothing more. I trust you shall do the same as your fellow knight."

She scowled. "Night falls. Let us kill this foul VVitch." As she started climbing once more, Brimeor followed, muttering: "The sailors have the right of it. Were the Evermeadow to pleasure itself with the frozen waters up north, surely we too would be wise to deny a woman passage aboard." He caressed the tuft of dried grass hanging from the pommel of his sword. Luckily for Rose's sanity, Haera didn't hear the Everknight's words.

"The wind is quiet no more," the Rosewood Knight commented as they reached the bottom of the mountainside, "The valley floor howls with the vengeance of a newly widowed. Listen as the black and gray branches rustle in harmony, creating waves of dark symphony."

"You mean listen for the VVitch," Haera realized. "Ill would be our fate should he catch us unawares."

They met marshy forest floor, spewing ancient foul vapors and fog, their feet sinking through the muck of green algae. It went deeper than they expected, and when they finally felt the bottom, it seemed as though the ground were floating, ready to swallow them up at any moment. Old bones stood vigilant. Skulls of deer, auroch, crow, and human, sunken in the water, and further along, mounted on sticks, tied with chains and the faint, green glow of candles emanating from them. They needed no light of their own to see the way.

When Brimeor saw the dead, he cursed. "VVitch knows we are here."

The Rosewood Knight pushed one of the altars into the swamp. "They are lich now, incapable of harm." The structure toppled, and yet, strangely, the green glow of the flames didn't extinguish.

"Whether these flames forever burn, or VVitch himself is welcoming us into his halls, it is surely a dark sign," Brimeor stated. "Listen to the forest. Do you hear any sounds of life? Nay, only that of watchers and forgotten things."

Haera shivered. "I like this not, Sirs."

Brimeor gave his best attempt at a laugh, and failed. It sounded strained, as if he himself did not wish to make himself too known. "We gave you a chance to turn back. You refused, and yet here you stand, up to your knees in muck and being the only voice of complaint."

Haera began to retort, when Rose held up his hand for silence. "Something wicked approacheth."

They heard it, too. It was a slow, steady sound. Barely heard underneath the rustling trees and whining wind. It rasped, as if giving one last breath before life was to be a distant memory. Ripples followed in its wake. Even in the pitch darkness, they could make it out, moving towards them in the water. The knights unsheathed their swords. The Rose's burned with fire etched in circles through the metal of his broadsword. It outshone those of the other two, who bore only simple longswords. Haera with a writhing kraken inscribed in the hilt and Brimeor's with his string of hay attached. Their weapons had been forged, passed down to them through generations. The Rosewood Knight's? His had been found.

The ground exploded underneath Haera. A plume of water shot into the air, momentarily engulfing the Selkie. Rose dared think she had perished for a split second, before he realized she was rising, and not drowning. Rising on the head of a giant serpent. Seaweed and muck clung to its slimy, green body. A forked, silver tongue licked the air through a mouth of dozens of small, white teeth. Around its scales, yellow eyes fumed with hate and hunger.

It thrashed, attempting to knock the lady off, who had spun her sword in the air and was balancing on top of it expertly, striking it with her blade. The hits emitted sparks as they bounced off the tough scales.

Sir Brimeor shouted something in his language and swung his sword at the end of its tail, occupied by black, beehive shaped parts. Whenever the serpent moved, those parts gave a low, steady rattle. However, his attacks seemed to be making just as much of an affect as Haera's. Rose met its fangs head on. It lashed out at him, snapping with razor sharp teeth. With the flick of a wrist, he sent one of the teeth flying, getting stuck in a tree trunk. Blood sprayed from its mouth. It gave a pained hiss, so loud that it almost sounded like a roar.

His companion understood. Giving up on cutting through the tough scales, he sprinted to the tree, and wrenched the fang loose. The serpent seemed to get it, too, and lunged at him. Brimeor gave a quick slash at its face, and it drew back, blinded in one eye. From the top of its head, Haera leaned down, stabbing her sword into its other eye, the weapon becoming lodged. It thrashed and screamed as loud as a snake could scream. She leapt off before it crashed backwards into the muddy waters.

"One eye, white as pearl and red as crustacean, the other crimson as kraken with the ship's prow protruding out of it," Brimeor noted, stepping back. He was invoking the words of the holy texts of his homeland. Rose knew that the knight had no room in him for such pretty speeches. Briefly, he wondered what story or god he was quoting, before brushing away the thought. It didn't matter. The gods must truly be blind for monsters like this to exist.

He stopped his mind from wandering too late. In a moment of negligence, his foot sunk down into the water, and broke through the bottom. The trees were growing larger around him. The reeds and smiling skulls became giants. He called for help, but the others were busy finishing off the creature, Brimeor almost hugging its slippery body as he tried to hold it down while it thrashed belly-up in the mud. Haera dug her sword from its bleeding eye, punching and kicking to get it to give its life to her. The snake and Rose wriggled and screamed, both dying.

The ground was around his shoulders now, his body freezing in the water that bogged down his armor. Something pulled him deeper with a huge tug. What light there was up above faded as he fell into the sea under the swamp. It was dark there. A silent, blackish-blue void. He saw a woman up above him. Black robes flowed just like her mass of curled, red hair. The woman's face was not skin, but made of the night sky itself, half obscured by a frowning mask made of white marble. Behind her, the stars were spinning, faster and faster, forming a circle which perfectly framed her body. *No. Not you.*

To get out, Rose had to swim toward her. Reach for her taunting embrace. *No matter*, he thought. *I won't die here. Not like this. I will go past her, and past her power.* He tried to move his arms, dig them into the water to try and go back up the surface. He kicked his legs, muscles moaning, lungs on fire, eyes stinging. His armor was like a rock tied around his ankles. Try as he might, he could only sink deeper.

She grew closer. The water flowed around her, like a robe's fabric in a breeze. She seemed to glow, only becoming brighter as the water was darker. In the black hole of her mask, Rose saw a well in a forest, in which he stared down to its depths. Inside, he saw death and decay. He saw a feast for buzzards and a rotten specter from an age long forgotten.

Then, he felt the hand grab him. He tried to grab it, make it let go. He wouldn't go with the woman. He would not. It was useless, though, as he went higher. Higher. Higher.

He broke the surface, and there the Rosewood Knight lay shamefully, spluttering and coughing up disgusting water. His helmet was still on, and it felt heavy as he looked to see who had rescued him. Haera stood before him, grinning. *How I hate that smile. That arrogant, boastful smile.* Too long had people trampled over Rose, pushing him into the mud, wearing that exact smile. Behind Haera, Brimeor screamed as he continued to stab the dead serpent. Rose wanted to join him. Really, really wanted to. To unleash his pent-up frustration on something that couldn't fight back. Instead, he put on a grateful smile, though none could see it.

He accepted her outstretched arm and pulled himself to his feet. "You saved my life, Lady Haera. Not all the pages of the Codex could express my wondrous gratitude."

She put her helmet back on. "Any knight would have done the same."

Brimeor strode over, head held high. He clasped Rose's arm. "Almost lost you."

Rose shrugged off the gesture. "I am alive, as we all are. This is the tool that will destroy VVitch. Life, fighting with the strength of the realm, against death."

Brimeor spread his arms, looking around the dark forest. "He should show himself, if he so delights in our misfortune! Do you hear me, VVitch?!"

Lady Haera grabbed his arm. "Fool! We hope to catch this dark wærlock unawares, no thanks to your babbling!"

The Everknight yanked himself free. "It is a harmless boast. VVitch is a coward, hiding in his hovel and spreading sorcery across the Heartlands. Now I see that his magyk is mortal."

The candelabras swelled across the bog. A thousand flames glaring at the party. The Rosewood Knight backed away as the one next to him spilled green cinders. Though his body hid behind a thick plate of armor, he didn't like the flames. They were too wild, unpredictable. Dangerous. They reflected off the water, causing shadows to spread across Haera and Brimeor's armor. He could have sworn he saw a shadow grinning at him on the Selkie's breastplate before all the flames collectively went out.

Cold wind blew the remaining smoke away, leaving them shivering in the dark. "He taunts us," Rose muttered.

"VVitch trickery this is, nothing more. I'll not have you become so hysterical as the woman," Brimeor stated. He sloshed deeper into the waters, apparently giving up on making their way across what little dry land there was to reach their target.

Sir Brimeor turned to look at them. He gave a cocky grin. "Come, we should keep mov-" As he was pulled underneath the water, the loudest noise he was able to make was a small splash.

Haera cursed in a loud whisper, as if she could barely stop herself from screaming. Rose took out his sword, the faint glow from it now the only bit of light around them. He went over to where Brimeor had sunken, careful not to stand on the exact on the spot, so as not to be pulled under himself. He had not much liked it the first time, but that had been an accident. A stupid place to put his foot. Brimeor hadn't done that. Brimeor had been purposely drowned.

"Was it another serpent?" Haera's voice hushed and slightly trembling.

He stared at the spot, a ripple still traveling across the water. Instead of answering her, he squinted. The water was getting darker. The air smelled salty-sweet, like metal. The Rosewood Knight nearly fell as something else rose out of the marsh, very, very slowly.

Haera doubled over, her gasp cut off with a stream of vomit. In the few seconds he had been gone, Brimeor had been strapped to a wooden post with the same chains that the candelabras bore. His mouth was twisted in a scream, helmet and armor lost. In his outstretched hand, his skin gray and covered with gooseflesh, was a rusted music box. The metal dug into his palm, creating a perfect square to rest in. The device had been turned on, the silhouette of a small marionette figurine spinning as a slow, eerie tune played in the dark. Blood dripped, staining the water. His leg had been torn off in a way that it had also taken his manhood. Sir Brimeor's eyes were rolled back, crying as the marsh drained out from the dead man.

The Rosewood Knight was fast to act. He shook the last remaining member of the party. "Get a grip of yourself! He's trying to scare us off. It must mean we're close. Come, let us put an end to this wickedness. VVitch dies before sunrise."

Haera fell to her knees, trembling. "He's dead. He's dead."

"Rosewood Knight…"

They looked. Brimeor's mouth was moving. His lips shook like someone from inside his mouth had stuck their fingers up his throat and was controlling him.

"Enter!" Cried the dead man, and then his jaw unhinged, and his mouth kept opening, opening, and opening. His teeth sagged and his gums bled as they became a doorway.

"Come," Rose whispered. "Be brave, Lady Haera."

Haera stared wide-eyed at the water. "He's dead. He's dead. Just… *Seilþalgr*, look at him!"

The Rosewood Knight wrapped his arms around hers, and began to pull her towards the entrance. She kicked the water, splashing and spraying with her flapping arms. She wailed. Loud. High-pitched. The shield mounted to the back of her chestplate glittered, the black paint showing the kraken, even at night. He wondered why it hadn't been painted red. Rose shoved her away in disgust. "You shame your title, *Sir* Haera. Very well, I shall avenge our fallen comrade on mine own."

She outstretched her arm, waiting for him to help her up, but it was too late. The Rosewood Knight had marched inside. Holding his sword in front of him, using its burning circles etched into the metal like a torch, he saw that the walls slowly began to change. What once resembled Brimeor's flesh had turned into stone, crumbling and moldy. Tongue turned to stairs beneath his feet, and he tried his best not to slip as they spiraled downward. The air stank of stale breath. The music box still played, though it was beginning to get drowned out by the sound of a beating heart. A steady beat, almost like a horn.

The sides of the walls had once been decorated with banners, now only small strips of cloth clinging onto iron rods, the color and imagery faded long ago. His gauntlet brushed against a brick that had been painted on, more recently than the banners, but still old enough that it was in poor condition. Despite the dim lighting, he could see the unmistakable red of a rose.

The Rosewood Knight counted fifteen of the heartbeats before reaching the bottom of the staircase. The steps ended abruptly before a short entry hall, where a wooden door lay in wait for him to open. Above the doorway, the image of a sun on top of a moon had been carved. When he blinked, the symbols switched, the moon on top and the sun below. Rose opened the door with a creak, surprised at finding it unlocked.

The space was tiny, almost enough so that he felt if the ceiling had been any lower, he would be forced to stoop. The round shape of the room made the space feel stuffy, not helped by a crackling hearth at the end. On a spit above it, a metal cauldron bubbled. Animal hides hung on the walls, brown and black and white. Some were still stained with blood, and the heads they belonged to had been mounted. Fangs, needle-like teeth, and horns looked at Rose. Various herbs, mushrooms, and bottled potions smelling sweet hung from the ceiling, jingling as he moved about the room. On the mantle of the fireplace, a jar containing an enormous pickled toad emanated a slight glow. Human skulls kept in alcoves carved into the stone grinned at the Rosewood Knight as he readied his stance, waiting for an attack.

If not for the heavy metal covering his broad shoulders, Rose would have felt the shriveled fingers creeping up to his neck sooner.

Whipping around, Rose slashed at the air, where the arm would've been. Instead, he cut nothing. "Your dark wings will no longer cast its shadow across the land," the Rosewood Knight called out. Somehow, his voice came out quieter than he'd intended.

The cauldron began to shake back and forth, until the pot tipped over, spilling onto the hard, stone floor. Intestines sloshed onto the ground, the grooves underneath filling with water and blood. Red and glistening, Rose knew they didn't belong to any animal. From inside, something was wriggling, causing the meat to move. Walking forward, Rose used one hand to move the intestines aside. They curled around his arm like a snake, until he crushed them beneath his metallic fingertips. Inside the remains was a newborn. It began to cry, pounding tiny fists into the air as its eyes were tightly shut, fused closed by crust. Its umbilical cord was still attached to something deep within the fleshy mass. Before the Rosewood Knight could decide what to do next, the newborn began to grow.

The head grew, so much so that it became too much for its body to handle and it hung limp around the neck, still wailing. The legs became long and hairy. The arms lost fat as they clutched at its stomach. The crying turned to moaning, then screaming, then laughing. VVitch stood up, pushing back greasy black hairs that clung to his mostly bald scalp.

"Knight of the Rosewood," He croaked, in a voice that was gravely and low, tainted by an otherworldly accent. "What think you of my new palace?"

The Rosewood Knight pricked the pale flesh of VVitch's chin with the point of his sword. Rose glanced up the stairs, wondering if Haera could hear them. "I'll have no more crude sorcery from you. Accept your death like a man, or meet Abyss like a coward."

VVitch's eyes narrowed. "You need me!" He hissed. His tongue resembled an eel, flicking between yellow, pointed teeth. "You'll rot without my magyks."

"The land rots *with* your magyk." Rose raised his weapon and brought it swinging, cleaving through VVitch's neck like carving a stick of butter. Blood sprayed across his helm. The severed head tumbled onto the ground.

The Rosewood Knight dragged the body to the fireplace and pushed it in, watching as it collapsed into a mass of wriggling maggots, screaming as they burned. "Why?" Asked the head, as he stooped to pick it up.

"Your blight chokes the earth, and roses smell sweeter than worms." The Rosewood Knight dropped it into the flames. The potion vials on the shelves and ceilings shone with the fire's reflection.

Haera was gone when he walked back up the stairs.

CHAPTER ONE

"Oh, my lady, my lady, my sweet Lady of Lerelei!" The Rosewood Knight called.

The princess's tower was made of a beautiful, sparkling white stone. A perfect circle of inlaid bricks, shining like a beacon in the Heartlands around them. They were the only structure not in ruins, unlike those hidden in the trees and grasses for miles around. This one was a work of art. It did not look as if it had been placed by man or marionette, but rather carved from a mountain, carefully chiseled to perfection. The mountain was gone, but the tower was not, and it would remain long after. Black, thorny vines accented the sides perfectly, as they curled around the lone structure. The pointed, purple tile roof began with a wide brim, slowly curving inwards until it ran with a smooth motion up to a point, where it held aloft a flag. On the fabric, a swan glided among the stars. Rose smiled.

A balcony occupied the top portion of the building. Made of marble, its banisters curled tight and ran along the length of the platform, weaving in between the vines, which were growing dazzling white flowers. Everything about the tower was perfect, even in its overgrown state. The sun glinted off the whiteness, so he kept his eyes focused beneath his helm on the princess walking out onto the balcony.

She parted a curtain of petals that hung in front of her doorway, and yawned. A nightgown covered her smooth, dark skin. Unbrushed, black hair was tangled around her bronze antlers. The lady of Lerelei smiled, white eyes widening. "Oh, my Rose! You have returned! I pray I sound unselfish with my words, but I had so wished it had been just moments later. The hour is early, and I should hate for you to gaze upon me so in my current state. My hair has not been tidied, my powders unapplied. I should hope you carry Sun-Bright words."

The Rosewood Knight kneeled in the lush red summer grass. "Your complexion needs no powders nor taming, my Lady Lorenna. Even a love potion could not strengthen the way I thinketh you, for my love is already at its most powerful. I do indeed bring joyous news. VVitch is slain.

No longer shall you need to remain in your spire. The land is untainted once more."

She spread her arms, spinning in a circle as she basked in the sunlight. After a moment, she paused, looking down at the Rosewood Knight. "Why, do I recall correctly that my Rose had two brave flowers accompany him on that valiant journey? Where might they be? I should like to give them my thanks. Think you a kiss each be an ample reward? Great treasuries of the realm?"

His smile faded. "I have not seen sweet Lady Haera since I spilt the blood of VVitch upon the earth. Sir Brimeor… Noble Sir Brimeor's death shook her, methinks."

The princess closed her eyes, vibrant blue tears sliding down her cheeks. "I had heard many a tale of his honor and courage. I hoped to gain the pleasure of knowing him better after your quest. I shall sing a song for him when the moon is full. Perhaps it will guide his spirit to rest. Tell me, good Sir, how did it happen?"

The Rosewood Knight paused. "I would not burden you with the grizzen details. Know that it was quick. As for your ballad, I would humbly ask that you refrain from it. The Evermeadow does not partake in such archaic beliefs. They will retrieve Brimeor and bury him in his homeland."

Though Rose's love for Lerelei was apparent, he thought that her gods derived power from belief. Her religion was an old one, and one which had overstayed its welcome. The Evermeadow and other places around the planet had already moved on, and it was high time that the Heartlands did as well. The Rosewood Knight didn't blame Lorenna for practicing her beliefs, as he imagined there wasn't much else to do in her situation. Ettiah of the Moon's Blood was not a merciful god. If the Codex didn't lie, as it had been written in the time when her religion was widespread, then blood sacrifices were not frowned upon. He wondered if Lorenna still practiced that, too.

She pursed her lips. "As you wish. My heart goes to his family, and to my dear Haera. May she return in safety." Lorenna sighed, leaning on the railing.

"My lady, I implore you to take care on the balcony. The fall is long and hard, and I would not wish you to be as broken as me in my attempts to gain your hand. Mine own shake in fear of your downfall. They tremble at the thought of your iridescent beauty, and your antlers as tall and elegant as the trees."

She laughed. Even the Rosewood Knight found it hard to put the sound into words. It was like the breeze from a cool summer rainfall, blowing gentle wind chimes. "Rise, my knight. What was more shocking than finding you climbing my tower at night for a visit, was that you stood up after your plunge into the rose bushes. It would make for a rather poetic end to your tale, would you not agree?"

It was Rose's turn to purse his lips, though the Lady Lerelei could not see beneath his helmet. "Let us hope that that end is far and long from this day, though mayhaps it would be a sweet death to gaze upon your features."

She blushed. "Let us speak no more of death. That is saved for the night, when Abyss laughs and the Moon's Blood is fullest." She held out her finger and a cardinal landed, singing a merry song. "It is a new day, and I must depart into my quarters to pray for Sir Haera's safe return to me. I would bear you farewell, my Rose, if I did not know better."

He gave a deep bow, grateful that his helm fit his head so perfectly. "I shall return on the morn, and the morn after that, and the one after that. I would defy a thousand lifetimes to win your hand, sweet maiden." The Rosewood Knight stood up. He waited for a breathless moment. "I must confess… I am not so brave as you deem me so." He walked back a few paces, so he could see Lorenna paused in her doorway, parting back a curtain of flowered vines. Rose had never been able to glimpse the inside of her tower.

"Why, from your own speech, it sounds as if you fought VVitch on your lonesome. What is that, I wonder, if not bravery of the highest order?"

"The night before, oh it shames me to say so, my princess, but on the night before I wept to the blackest of dreams! Black, awful dreams. Of treachery and trickery. What made my heart cry was discovering you at the center of this foulest of plots, my Lady Lorenna of Lerelei. Not as the plotter, oh no, you are far too kindly and innocent to be capable of that. You were the target. The planned victim of dark deeds done in the name of spite and greed. I fear…" Rose waited. "No. I darest not say."

She gasped, lifting a hand to her mouth. "Say it! Let it slip between your teeth. If I am in danger I must know from what or whom!" The cardinal took off with a small, annoyed chirp.

The Rosewood Knight hung his sentence in the air for a split sentence, before uttering: "Filicide."

Lorenna's expression tightened just as hard as her jaw. "You mean to say…? No. My mother would never do me harm. Never."

"I implore you, think on it, my lady. If the ruler of the greatest House Lerelei should have her daughter marry a mere vagabond knight, his house almost unheard of in the Heartlands, she would think great shame upon her family. If she cannot force you to join hands with someone else, there is only one other solution."

Lorenna Lerelei walked inside, yet her cold words hung in the air as if she were still on the balcony. "I have not agreed to marry you just yet, Rosewood Knight. I would think on that before choosing your next words the day next."

He stood there, looking at his boots in the red grass. His breathing echoed as they came out of the metallic helmet. Angling his head upward, he stared at the sky, now violet with the sun having risen more. The breeze felt too warm. It annoyingly tugged at his cloak and made him sweat underneath his suit of armor. *Like a streetwalker in prayer.* With a sigh, he turned and walked to his steed, tied to an old fence post by a clump of dandelion trees.

Windsoar was a marionette, modeled after a statzal, with powerful legs worked by bronze gears peaking above its hindquarters. Its hooves left weird prints in the soil, full of waving lines and surrounded by a checkered pattern. Its tucked wings were taken directly from the beast it was inspired from, consisting of a shimmering, insectile-like thin material surrounded by a black outline of exoskeleton that crept into the center like veins or tree branches. It snorted, the furnace inside Windsoar's rib cage flaring, glowing red all the way to its nostrils on its snout, which puffed out hot steam. The Rosewood Knight had attempted to cover the slits in its wood-like body with metal plating, but each time the pressure had proved too great, and he had been forced to remove it or suffer a marionette torched from the inside out. That would not do, as to his knowledge this was the only steed of its kind in existence.

That would prove obvious to anyone who happened to look upon him as he snapped the reins, making lots of mechanisms to click into place and cause the mount to lift its head. Then it ran. It ran faster than any horse that could be found wandering the land. It thundered with quick precision. It never got tired, and although appearing as if it ate the grass, Rose found out that the vegetation burned inside its stomach, proving useless as it didn't need food or drink. As it galloped, it spread its wings, fluttering them at such rapid speeds that it seemed as though the knight of the Rosewood was surrounded by a hypnotizing blur. Though its body was too big for permanent flight, it did glide off the ground for seconds at a time, pushing the wind in its favor to achieve greater speeds.

Windsor was much faster and more powerful than regular statzels, which his mechanical design was inspired by. Statzels roamed the Midnight Sea coast and outskirts of the Heartlands in herds, resembling horses with bug wings and gray skin. With Windsoar underneath and his blade, *Last One*, in his hand, Rose felt invincible.

The landscape would not change unless he reached the Midnight Sea or crossed the rainbow mountains, Rose knew. *Someone from the Evermeadow or Willowood would think it a hellscape of magnificence*, he had once heard Lorenna say, as she looked at the crimson tallgrass and the odd grove of white dandelion trees. Their seeds filled the air, creating gray flocks against the purple sky, becoming invisible whenever a pink cloud blocked out the sun. If the seeds landed in the grasses, they would likely be smothered by the vegetation, unable to grow. The Rosewood Knight reckoned that was why there were so few of them fully blossomed, though he expected a forest of them would be unkind, to say the least, on his nostrils.

Running beside him, a herd of enormous gray rabbits bounded against the ground, their noses twitching and ears flopping in the wind. Rose found himself wondering a lot why he hadn't bothered to tame one of them, until he saw their barbed tongues licking sharp, yellow teeth. It was for the best, in any case. Rabbits got tired. Marionettes didn't, and weren't carnivorous, either. He gripped the hilt of his sword, though he didn't expect them to go for the fast-moving target that he was.

Finally, when the beams of light reflecting off his armor signaled midday, Rose arrived at his keep, just in time for lunch. *One could hardly call this a keep. A real lord would choke on his mead laughing should they look at it*, he thought bitterly. It was surrounded by a low wall of untrimmed hedges, easily burned, easily climbed through. The ground was filled with mud and dying grass, though he had ordered his castellan to have it paved, the ancient marionette apparently hadn't gotten around to it yet, or maybe forgotten about it entirely. Potential attackers could possibly slip on the muck and break their necks, though it was not of much use for anything else, except for reminding him of his poverty. The structure itself was the worst part. He had found it overgrown and ridden with vermin, and it had not changed much since he had arrived. Try as they might, the Rosewood Knight and his castellan could not improve the top half leaning precariously to one side, the ivy growing like weeds in between the bricks, the rodents scurrying about from their hidden lairs.

Leading Windsoar into the stables he had built purely from the stems of the dandelion trees and his own sweat and blood, he swung the stall shut and was met by the Castellan. Peering outside from the peeling oak door into the keep, the Castellan resembled a stick insect, with plating the same texture as Windsoar, though painted silver, red, and gold to match Rose's colors. He shambled outside, pressing two sets of hands together as the third pair folded behind his back. He wore a black velvet suit vest with a dark-red handkerchief and a golden pocket watch. It was the only set of clothing fit for a servant they had found that hadn't been eaten by moths. A metal wind up key erupted from the marionette's back, endlessly turning. Covering half of his face was a smiling, white marble mask.

"My lord, words cannot describe my relief upon witnessing his safe return." His voice came out echoey and scratched, like it came out of a tin can. "Please, please, follow me! I have prepared proper sustenance for my lord. I imagine he is famished."

The Rosewood Knight stooped to enter the doorway. He didn't know if he was abnormally taller than whoever had originally had it built or if they were just short. He supposed it would have made no difference to them, or to the Castellan who had no such difficulties getting through, as his shoulders were always slightly hunched in any case. Feeling a disgusting taste in his mouth, Rose thought back to the cramped space of VVitch, but this memory vanished with the rumbling in his stomach. He realized he hadn't eaten since he had entered the forsaken valley. Rose carefully took off his helm and started shoveling heaps of steaming rabbit stew into his mouth. It had taken a considerable amount of effort to kill one of the beasts, but after salting, the Rosewood Knight had enough meat to last him for at least a fortnight to come. He winced whenever the spoon touched his lips, but he kept eating anyway. The seasoned, chewy meat was almost enough to cover the taste of the metallic spoon.

The Castellan watched him carefully. "If I may be so bold… how did your travels fare? Did you vanquish the VVitch? I have heard not of Sir Brimeor and Haera."

The Rosewood Knight placed down his utensil and sighed. "VVitch is slain."

The marionette bounced up and down in a circle, croaking, "Oh, well done, my lord! Well done indeed! I trust everything went according to plan, then?"

"Yes," Rose lied. He pushed his bowl away. "That's as much gruel as I can stomach for the time being, I think. I am off to my chambers."

The Castellan bowed, removing the bowl from the plain table draped in a sad off-white tablecloth. "And what does my lord bid me do whilst he is in slumber? Trim the hedges? Feed Windsoar? Fetch your bandages?"

Rose waved his hand as he climbed the flight of small, spiral stone stairs, helmet in hand. "No, not for the time being. Perhaps you could finally rid yourself of that ridiculous mask, however." It reminded him too much of her. The woman in the water.

The Castellan wrung his free hands. "Would that I could, my lord, would that I could. I am afraid this fixture is too greatly secured. Removing it may damage my machinery." His uncovered face was frowning, yet the mask was beaming.

Rose grunted and continued climbing up the stairs. His room occupied the top of the small tower, crowning the already small keep. The ceiling beams were higher than that of VVitch, but not by a considerable amount. He cursed at the comparison, undoing the straps of his armor and sending them clunking onto the floor. A poor reflection of Tower Lerelei, indeed. He placed his helm on a small bedside table. Groaning, the Rosewood Knight soaked a washcloth in a small wooden bowl and placed it over his brow, flopping onto the mattress.

Through his pounding head, he thought back to Lorenna Lerelei. He had been younger when he first met her, though it wasn't more than a few years ago. He had been more foolish, he thought, but still full of pretty words and vibrant songs. Mostly Rose remembered the flag flapping in the breeze. The princess yawning and exiting her tower room, the sunlight exposing her figure through her thin gown. Rose had thought she was blind, at first, beholding her white, wide eyes. She did, however, see him.

"Why, if you are not the lady of most noble births, then I am kneeling in front of none other than White Swan herself. Though your beauty is enough to make any other wonder turn to ash in my eyes for a hundred years, doth you a name? I should like to continue about my travels and tell all I meet of this spectacular thing before me."

She giggled. "Why, my sweet knight, I am Lorenna Lerelei, of the smallest blade of crimson grass to the puffiest dandelion tree and the tallest mountain." The Lady Lerelei gave a curtsey. "You have the honor of addressing the princess of the Heartlands. Oh, how I should relish in leaving this spire of mine to see you closer, but alas, it is not to be. My lady mother hath forbidden it so."

The Rosewood Knight stood up. "Then up to you, I shall go."

Another laugh. "Good Sir, how doth I bid a stranger to mine quarters without even a name to utter? Speak, warrior! What are the Heartlands to call you?"

"I am but the humble knight of the Rosewood, my lady. Passing through these lands for glory and honor, as is the tradition for knights of smaller birth who have little to rule over."

"Why, my Rosewood Knight, I am afraid I have played a poor jest on you. Just as I cannot exit my chambers, no one may enter. Should you walk the perimeter of this tower of mine, you will find no door nor entrance from which to open."

He felt cold. Rose was not fond of jokes. However, his composure was kept polite. "Very well. I passed many a plagued crop field and tainted water. Mayhaps these ever-barren lands have need of my presence for a time. If you so wish it, your house has my sword, through plight and strife."

"You honor me, Knight of Roses. If you so wish, dark words and whispers fly with the wind, of a lichen shadow to the north. Indeed, 'tis the reason why I am forbidden from leaving, so." She looked around, slightly covering her mouth, as if just saying it would incur unwished ears. Her next words were barely more than a whisper, so much so that he had to tilt his brow upwards to better listen. “A foul sorcerer, by the title of VVitch.”

The Rosewood Knight’s memories had somehow faded into dream. Pleasant at first, then diving deep into terrible nightmares. When he awoke, covered in sweat, the sun’s rays enveloped him through the broken shutters. Morning had come, but with no sleep, nor promise of matrimony on the horizon.

CHAPTER TWO

"Haera," Lorenna sighed, plucking a flower from the vine near the window. She let it fall between her fingers, into a cup of water. There it floated, never sinking, never wilting.

She spun in place, disturbing the kaleidoscope of pink butterflies on her antlers. Lorenna spread her arms, imagining the group of flying insects were a pair of wings, forever flying her away from her tower. The butterflies fluttered around her, tickling her skin, until they swam in a cloud of color into the sky. "Where art thou? What accursed thing did the VVitch inflict on you, to make you run away from me, so? My fearless Sir, always so brave. Mayhaps that foul wærlock has hidden you away. I have never known you to run from danger. Always so proud and mighty, in your gleaming armor, wind pulling at your hair."

There was a herd of pale deer grazing far below her, and she leaned her head against the marble railing in a dream-like ecstasy. The sun beamed down on her back, making her black hair feel like bread freshly out of the oven. How she loved freshly baked bread! Whenever she awoke, there would be a different meal awaiting her on the small, yellow table next to her bed, on a green, wooden tray. Occasionally Lorenna received a white, juicy plum with fruit tea and potatoes with scrambled eggs. Sometimes she even found a steaming bowl of brown, honeyed porridge with sausages on the side and a goblet of rich, sweet-tasting milk. Out of all the countless different meals, however, she loved slices of baked bread with a variety of jams, honeys, and butter displayed for her to lather on the meal as she wished. The warm butter dripping down her hands and chin was messy and scrumptious. The meal was simple, perhaps too much so for a princess, but somehow always the most filling.

Lorenna longed to share that bread with her dear friend. Anyone, really, even the Rosewood Knight, whose appearance had become a daily occurrence. Yet Mater bid no one into her chambers. It was a circular bedroom, complete with a queen-sized bed containing a blue canopy, in which grape vines curled their mighty bodies around its posts. Bookshelves filled with leather volumes covered the red wallpaper, displaying blooming flowers. On one side of the room, across the green carpet, a curtained section contained her lavish powder room, with a bathtub so deep she thought it might reach the bottom of the spire.

Birds yellow, blue, and red flew in and visited her. Unlike the butterflies, the Lady of Lerelei had to take care not to let the lively little things onto her antlers, lest they make nests for themselves. Apart from them, she was also fond of the mice that lived in between her books, who lived off the bits of cheese she allowed them to nibble on. At first it had been to keep them from eating the paper, but now she simply enjoyed their company.

Sometimes her mater visited. At least, Lorenna thought so. Who else would leave her food at night and behind her back during the day when she wasn't looking? She also thought the woman she saw in her dreams occasionally wasn't in her dreams at all. It was an unsettling feeling, though she never felt unsafe. Lorenna felt… protected. Protected, yes, but still it did not quiet her loneliness.

"Thoughts flutter like wings of a… well…" She sighed to herself, a butterfly perching on her outstretched finger. Lorenna wore a strapless dress ending in light pink puffs. She loved the color white, and her mater seemed to know it. She always found all manner of new gowns and dresses in her wardrobe, though it never seemed to run out of space. The princess laughed to herself. "Whatever shall I wear on my day of wedding, I ponder? My suitor must not see me in the same color on a day like that, oh no, no, no."

Lorenna shrieked as the cuckoo clock alarmed, spewing a whimsical, purple fox that ran in circles as the hour hand pointed toward luncheon. She covered her mouth. "Oh, how silly of me!" Looking at the empty table, she sighed. "Yes, yes. How could I have forgotten?" Turning around, she stared back at the vast, flat land. She sang a song as she waited for the meal to appear. It never wanted to if she was looking, as if it would spoil some secret. As much as Lorenna suspected her mater of somehow being responsible for this phenomenon, she could never prove it. It seemed the love for a daughter had its limits, as no matter how hungry Lorenna might be, the food would not come to her if she was looking. As she sang, the birds grew excited, fluttering around her. She smiled and cupped a green one in her palms, singing with all her heart now. She quite enjoyed music. It was a thing of which she had grown accustomed to as a form of entertainment.

The best kinds of entertainment, however, were when her friends came to visit. Lorenna had hoped that Brimeor could have proven a true friend, though he seemed to long only for his blade. His gruff demeanor had been one she had hoped to break through, but she was never given the chance. Lorenna was not sure what the Rosewood Knight had seen in him. Had. Her singing faded. *Please. Do not make it so dear Haera has met the same gruesome fate as Sir.* The bird seemed to sense her sudden change in mood and hopped onto her shoulder, nuzzling its soft head against her cheek.

She looked at her curious little green friend, then to the smoke rising far in the distance. "Do you think Mater will let me visit the fair this year? The marionettes passing through told me of all the curious new thing they have added, and it sounds delightful. I've been so good. She must let me." Lorenna took a cautious step onto the railing. Would this be the day that she would be able to escape? It would be a simple thing. Just as the Rosewood Knight had scaled the vines up, so would she down. Immediately the vines came to writhing life, snatching her ankle and forcing it back down onto the floor. She sulked, remembering all the Rosewood Knight's great falls in attempting to reach her quarters.

Tapping her foot impatiently, Lorenna decided she had waited long enough, and turned around. In front of her lay her food on the same table, on the same tray. Roast duck laden with cranberry sauce, surrounded by white rice, and a pitcher of wine on the side. Though food was one of the few joys she found she still enjoyed, today it tasted like the dust that choked the air when too many riders came through. The Heartlands had no roads to speak of, and so the odd traveler was forced to make their own trail. Many a crafty marionette sold information on which paths were to be avoided, for they held too many rabbits, and Lorenna expected they made a pretty coin of it, too. The long grass always grew back when steeds and feet crushed it. She wondered if she could say the same of herself.

Though she had a dining table, Lorenna preferred to dine on her balcony. She felt freest there. Away from her stuffy tower chambers. Looking over the wild scape, it felt good to be outside, so close to the enchanted life of a wanderer, like her Rosewood Knight. Yet, it stung, to be so close. It stung that her knights had that absolute freedom, to see the planet of all its wonders, and she did not.

It had been so long since Lorenna had seen Mater. Truly seen her, not in the shadows of her night-fallen bedroom. She dimly remembered herself as a babe bouncing on mother's knee. She had a different home, then. *She* had been different. As the princess grew older, so had mother's fears, and she had been sent away to her tower, free from the growing power of VVitch.

That was taken care of, now. The VVitch was felled, and yet still Lorenna could not leave. With all his promises, Rose had been unable to rescue her.

The Rosewood Knight was fair to look upon, 'twas true. At least, from what she could tell. He had broad shoulders, and powerful enough forearms to heave his great sword. Though she could name any gift she could think up, and he would bring it to her, he would not remove his helm, not with all the pleas she could give. Lorenna liked to imagine that he would take her to the Rosewood, should they marry. A magical place full of rose trees and streams that sang. He would hold her in his arms, and she would smell his sweet scent. He would take off his helmet, and together they would kiss until it grew too chilly to remain outside any longer. Color once again rushed to her face. It felt queer to have someone love her.

Nay, she thought to herself. *If he accuses my mater of… vile things, I shall not acknowledge him. Think not of him! His words were unjust, not one of a knight.* She misliked Mater at times, yes, but Lorenna believed Mater would never go as far as to kill her. *She still loves me. The food and clothing are proof enough of that.*

Lorenna finished the food on her plate. Looking up at the sky, she called: "Mater, why don't you trust me, so? I was a wee one when you took me, free of any wrongdoing. At least, I think so. My faint memories feel full of joy and free of sorrow, what changed, besides mine own flesh? I am certain I was safe from those who would do me harm there. Where you are now." A blue squirrel leapt onto the railing. She stroked the soft fur on its two tails. "But perhaps that was all it took. Your daughter dared grow up."

Feeling a rush of fury, she took the plate, feeling her fingernails scraping the surface, and flung it into the air. The squirrel chittered angrily and ran away. Lorenna Lerelei watched the object sail into the air, before shattering against the ground far away, pieces of the glass splintering across soil and rock and vegetation. Breathing heavily, it took Lorenna a moment to realize that it had begun to rain. Big, powerful raindrops that splashed onto her antlers and dripped into her eyes and cheeks. The flowers on the vines closed, shrinking away from the water as if its life force was not meant to touch their petals. Her body was shaking. Her throat ached. The rainwater tasted salty.

"Pardon me, fair lady." A voice quipped from the ground. It sounded high-pitched, like a child. Sniffing and wiping her face, she looked over the side. A marsh frog peered up at her. It was short, wearing a white linen sheet that covered its features, save for two holes roughly cut for its small, rounded ears to poke out of the top of its head, and two more for its yellow eyes to peer through. "I was a mere passerby when I could not help but hear your distress. Might there be anything I can do to help?"

She smiled at its sheer innocence. The marsh frogs lived in the dandelion tree groves dotted about the Heartlands. At dusk, Lorenna could often make out their small shapes darting in and out of the tree line just in front of her tower. They were reclusive creatures, and if one ever made the attempt to talk to her just as this one had, it was not by accident. Looking at the frog's curious head tilt, however, Lorenna knew its intentions were nothing but pure. "Nay, little frog. I'm afraid not. Not unless you can find someone brave enough to free me from this tower. I thought I had it… with my Rose, but it seems even he is not capable. He took many a fall, and I fear another could end him."

"Oh. I am sorry to hear that. Are you comfortable? Have you need of any provisions?" It bounced on its feet, looking towards the local grove of trees. She followed his line of sight, and saw more of his friends waiting for him, hidden amongst the bushes and rocks. Funny little creatures, those marsh frogs were. It seemed the people of the Heartlands felt great need to never reveal their features.

"How very kind of you. No. I have not much to complain of, up here, so close to the clouds. You are noble for asking. Should I ever feel the ground with mine own feet, come to me and I shall reward you for your kindness. I do have need for a new knight."

Its eyes became even larger. "Oh! I would like that very much!" It picked up a stick and swung it, slicing the air with triumphant thrusts and parries. "I've been practicing."

"Morrel!" Another frog called in a hushed, loud voice. "Come on, then. We've been waiting!"

"Coming!" Morrel called back. It started to run back, then bounced on its feet, looking at her. It made a hasty bow, then retreated to the grove. Lorenna watched as it joined its companions, laughing and dancing and playing make pretend, slaying shadowy dragons in the trees and many a fearsome ogre.

I should count myself lucky. Hardly anyone ever caught glimpse of the reclusive marsh frogs. She should be grateful for the comforts she had, as well. In the books she had, many prisoners did not have the same amenities she had grown used to having. That was how most of her days concluded, she found. Tired resignation. Resignation that nothing would ever change, and Lorenna would spend the rest of her days trapped in her tall spire, counting her blessings instead of her curses. Forced to watch others frolic and live their lives.

Darkness came. The stars danced among ribbons of green and blue. A choir of crickets sang their song, and Lorenna's white eyes grew tired. She sighed, feeling a sense of renewal after her stream of tears. Something flapped its wings overhead, and she could almost feel the breeze generated by its wings.

The wind swayed the vines that grew on her tower, tugging on them violently, as if the Rosewood Knight himself was attempting yet another ascent. A group of dandelion seeds were blown into the sky, illuminating the ash-like substance creating spirals in front of the Moon's Blood. The celestial body was a magnificent silver, round and beautiful, even with the deep black rivers running along its surface. The rivers were jagged and spreading, giving the appearance of a shattering great and terrible. Looking for any excuse to distract herself, she focused on the rustling there, on the planet, in her spire. The vines pulled and pulled, and Lorenna realized that someone *was* climbing them.

A figure, concealed by a cloak made black by the night. They planted their boots firmly on the white bricks, pulling their body upwards with each tug of the makeshift rope. Thorns cut into their palms, causing small streams of blood to drip down their arms, but they seemed to pay it no bother save the grunts of effort it took for them to make such a climb.

"Who's there?" Lorenna Lerelei called. *'Tis the nighttime chill that makes my voice waver. My hands shake. Indeed, it must be, for a princess feels no fear. The Heartlands are a hard place, and any hesitation yields you a victim to the wilds.* She tried to straighten herself. "State your name and business!"

They kept climbing, emitting heavy breathing, uttering naught but the word of the wind. Lorenna backed away into the fire-lit confines of her chambers, drawing the thin curtain that usually took up the space above the entrance to the terrace. Looking for a weapon and finding none, she settled on the bedpan, standing beside the door frame and holding it raised, thin arms trembling. She willed herself to speak again.

"M-my Rose? Could that be you? 'Tis not a good jape, Sir. You have never succeeded in the perilous climb in moons past, and I do not wish to see you injured more than you already have. I can still hear you climbing, scraping your feet along the stones. Are you cross? Did my last parting words offend thee? I am sorry. I grew… frustrated. 'Tis true, I have conflicted feelings for mater o' mine, but she never would… no, I do not believe she would ever harm me. I understand, now, oh, I do. You were just looking out for me. You care for me deeply, and– Oh, what a sour jape you are performing, knight! A sour jape indeed!"

The figure was on the other side of the curtain, now. Their dark, humanoid shape outlined by the moon. They had succeeded. They had climbed the tower. They were making a sound. It was laughter. "I am sorry, my princess!"

The vines were pushed aside. Not harshly, so that they would be ripped from their very stems, but soft. A curtain of flowers parting for Haera to glide through. Looking around, she spotted Lorenna sporting the bedpan, and slowly raised her arms. "Please, accept my humblest of apologies." Haera knelt. Lorenna lowered her weapon. "My journey has been long and treacherous. When I left the VVitch's forest, climbed over the jagged mountains, and staggered across these red lands, I faced many a horrid foe. Through my, I admit, somewhat delirious state, I thought up my encounter with you, and this was my bright conclusion. I see now I have frightened you terribly. Fear not, my lady, for I have eaten and drank, polished my armor, brushed my hair, and my mind has cleared. It was wrong of me to scare you, so. 'Twas a sour jest indeed. I apologize."

Lorenna had calmed down. She took Haera's hand and brought her to her feet. "All is forgiven, noble Sir. Please, rest by the roaring fire. You must be weary. My soul sings to see you return to me safely." They embraced, and she watched as the Selkie drew her cloak and took off her helm, swinging her head of hair to its full volume. Inexplicably, her heart began to beat faster again.

Haera sighed, sitting in an armchair next to the hearth. She faced her palms toward the fire. "As does mine, seeing you after so long. Oh, I know it has only been a day, but it has felt much longer."

Lorenna laid a hand on her. "My dear Haera, whatever happened? I heard about the fate of Sir Brimeor. My Knight of Roses would not go into detail, though I could tell that a terrible fate had befallen him. I was worried that something of that nature had happened to you! My Knight of the Midnight Sea, I know not what I would have done if you had made me wait longer. Just look at you now, all pale and shaken, staring into the flames as if you have witnessed terrible Abyss themself."

Haera looked at Lorenna. She shifted her arm so she their hands were linked. "I saw many an evil thing that night, but the most terrifying was not the death of Brimeor, nor the Rosewood Knight, nor VVitch. It was myself. I ran when I should have fought. Flown when I should have stood. I was a coward, too shaken to do what needed to be done. For days I wandered the Heartlands, even my steed abandoning me in my shame. During those days, Lorenna, I had time to think. I thought of what was important to me. Was it truly my pride? Was that what mattered most to my beating heart? No, I decided. It was something else. If I couldn't protect my people, even those I held contempt for, how could I hope to fight for those I loved?" Haera's eyes were a deep shade of green, so, so soft as they looked at each other. "I stopped once to bathe in a stream, though I was weak from exhaustion. I needed the flowing strength of Seilþalgr with me. In his protective embrace, I made a promise. I promised that I would never run again. Not ever. No matter how much the Rosewood Knight may make me wish to, I will always be there for you. For the one I love most." She got up and kneeled before Lorenna, one knee on the floor and the other supporting her elbow. "This is my vow, Lorenna of Lerelei."

Lorenna smiled sadly. She took hold of Haera's hand once more and helped her to her feet. She was so close that Lorenna could almost feel her warm chest. "I… I know not how to express my gratitude. In all my life, never have I been moved by such words. I daresay no poet or playwright could match your powerful declaration. However, I wish not to sour your speech, but I ask you, what is the point?" She gestured about the room. "I will never escape my imprisonment. I will never walk amongst the trees and fields of the land. I will not feel the soft grass betwixt my feet, nor a lover's embrace underneath the shining sun and the cool breeze, nor the cold steel of sword by those who would harm me." She felt her eyes well with tears again. "Mayhaps you should leave and live your life. Do not worry for me. I can marry the Rosewood Knight and live a happy-enough existence. I wish only the same for you, not bound to a fate of chore rather than pleasure."

Haera placed her hands on Lorenna's shoulders. "My lady, I had the chance to see the world. I wandered from the great sea to these empty plains to the towering rainbow mountains. I saw what your heart wishes to see, and at the end, the only thing I wanted was to come back to your tower and see you. I need not the oath of Seilþalgr to know truth. I do not want you to marry the Rosewood Knight. I want you to be with me. If you spend the rest of your life in this tower, doing the same thing every single day, I would be happy if I was with you."

Lorenna leaned forward and kissed her. She wrapped her arms around Haera's waist as they fell into the movement. Her heart seemed like it was dancing along with the flames in the fireplace, and for the first time that day, she felt an incredible rush of happiness.

CHAPTER THREE

Morrel the marsh frog was going to become a knight! Bouncing on his feet, he could barely keep the excitement from gushing out of him as he joined his friends.

Daeyvon was the tallest of the group, and he stared down at Morrel like he had grown a third toe. "You talked to her?"

They were well within the grove now, sundown falling down through canopies of dandelions. Even though just a few trees were between them and the outside world, it seemed like a big wall kept them inside. Or, as the other marsh frogs viewed it, safe from everything else. Morrel didn't know what they were so scared of.

"The princess said she was to make me a knight!" He finally let out, the words tumbling out of him in a jumble.

Morrel's friends stared at him. Daeyvon, who was the tallest, Cadissa, the one who could jump the highest, and Daniel, the quietest. All three of them wore the white sheets that the marsh frogs were stitched from birth, acting as cozy blankets at night, protecting them from the wilds of the Heartlands. Not even Daniel could keep in a giggle as the other two burst into laughter.

"A knight? You?" Cadissa managed out as she hugged her stomach. "Remember when you were scared to go into the pond? What'd you say was in there? Selkies?"

Morrel glanced over to the pond they were talking about. Shaded by the trees overhead, it was a favorite spot for the four of them during the summertime, but when he was littler, he thought he had seen a face in the water, smiling at him. For an entire fortnight, no one could convince him to dip one foot into the water. It finally ended when Mum grabbed him by the collar of his sheet and tossed him in for a much-needed bath.

He cleared his throat, straightening himself. "Every knight has fears to conquer."

"That's true," Daeyvon considered. "Didn't your granddad travel across the land? Who knows what he faced out there?"

Morrel crossed his arms. By now his friends had quit giggling. He knew it was all in good fun. Actually, all four of them were far more adventurous than the rest of the frogs in their grove, much to their parents' displeasure. He was the youngest in the group, so was usually the most teased. Not that much younger, however. Just a year or so shy of the others.

They wound their way around a large, moss-covered boulder, and slipped into a crack in the stone. The cool air immediately washed over them, a sweet release from the humid day, and the tunnel began to widen and flatten, turning into the cozy cavern they called home. Roots twisted their way out of the walls, budding moss carpeting the ground and a small stream trickling against the wall. Lichen faintly glowed, giving them just enough light to make their way to their homes. One by one, Morrel's group split off, going home to the smaller burrows inside of the cave. Eventually, it was just Morrel and Daeyvon left.

His friend glanced over. "She really said she'd make you a knight?"

Morrel nodded, glancing nervously around. He didn't want any of the adults to overhear that he'd been out of the grove again. In a whisper, he said: "When that curse of hers goes away. You know that red knight we've seen hanging around? Apparently he hasn't been able to fix it."

Daeyvon's eyes grew wide. "If he can't even cure her, how will she ever escape that tower?" He huffed. "Don't know how she can stand it. No trees, no grass beneath her toes. I think I'd go mad."

"Well, now, Daeyvon, you're starting to sound like our parents," Morrel teased.

"Yeah, yeah," he stopped. Morrel and he were the only frogs still up and about. Faint laughter and music could be heard from the burrows around them, including Daeyvon's. "You're not really gonna do it, are you? Become a knight?"

Morrel looked at him. "I thought you'd understand, Dae. We always try to go outside of the grove. You and I know we can't stay here forever, no matter how much our parents say so."

"Yeah…" He shifted his feet. "I should be getting home. I'll see you in the morning, Morrel."

His friend slipped into his home, and Morrel was all alone. *Why's he suddenly got such cold feet?* He found himself wondering. *We go outside all the time. Especially this time of year, when the fair comes around.* The fair attracted all sorts around the Heartlands. Morrel had always begged his parents to go, and they always said no. Going meant food, carnival games, and of course, marionettes. They were the funnest to talk to, since they sometimes came near the grove. They told the frogs stories of the outside world, like the VVitch in the north.

A terrible sorcerer, legend had it that he came from another planet out amongst the stars. No one could figure out why he spread plague and disease, except for the fact that he seemed to like it. Like it just as much as Morrel loved his mum's stew. In fact, he could smell it from here, and he hurried home. A bowl of mushroom stew with floating chunks of pepper and potatoes sounded like just the meal to celebrate the first step in becoming a knight. Not that Mum could ever know. Moon's Blood knew what she'd do.

His burrow was at the very end of the long cave, nestled on the other side of a tuft of thin dandelion roots, red and gnarled. He brushed them aside, and wove his way in a tight stone corridor. The light from a fire got brighter, until he was standing inside his home. He quickly wiped his feet on a welcome mat, before stepping onto a warm, wool carpet that covered the ground. A tree stump made a table on one side of the round room, with two smaller ones acting as seats. Two hammocks woven from lush, green vines hung on opposite ends of the space, looking on the blazing fireplace with a bubbling pot spit over the fire.

It would've been good to take a bowl of stew, sit in front of the fireplace, and slowly doze off until he crawled onto his hammock to sleep. It would've been great, even, if Mum wasn't standing directly in front of him. Arms crossed, clutching a wooden ladle, her apron in front of her white sheet, it didn't take a genius to guess that she was *crossed.*

"Mum-" Morrel began, before she knocked him on the head with her instrument of death and cooking. "Ow," he replied, rubbing the sore spot.

"*Morrel,*" she hissed. "Care to tell me what Daniel's mother saw you four doing today?"

He winced. Daniel always squealed, he just didn't think it would be so soon. Usually, they had a few days of peace before there was Abyss to pay. "Catching firebugs?" He tried, then quickly hopped back to avoid another swing from her.

"Don't you dare lie to me! You went outside the grove again. Not only that, but you talked to someone!"

"I didn't step five meters beyond the tree line, and the princess is nice! I didn't tell her no secrets!"

She drew back. "The princess? Oh, 'scuse me, your radiance, I didn't realize you had an audience with her majesty. I suppose I'll just excuse you for disobeying me time and time again, especially considering what happened to your grandfather."

Morrel's grandfather had been the only marsh frog to venture outside of the grove, and to top it all off, he never came back from his travels into the unknown. Wild rumors were still whispered about him to this day, from becoming a pirate captain on the Midnight Sea, to being crowned king of the planet. Morrel always loved hearing those stories. It made him feel special, being related to the old man, and made it seem possible to leave on an adventure of his own one day. Mum would have none of it, of course. She had already accepted him as long dead, so her paranoia only grew of the outside world.

He knew there was no reasoning with her. Trying in the past had only resulted in no soup for the night, and Morrel wouldn't wish that on his worst enemy. Trying to look sorry, he hung his head. "I'm sorry, Mum."

"Oh, no you don't. There'll be no more puppy eyes from you." She marched over to the wall and picked up a small, flat disk from a ledge, no bigger than Morrel's palm. It was a transceiver, something which all the grown-up frogs had to talk with each other without being in the same room. They had found a big pile of them generations ago and kept them. Morrel was pretty sure no one else had anything else like them in the Heartlands, though they weren't very useful outside of gossip, since they didn't work about three hundred yards out from the grove. "I just talked to all your friend's mums and da's, and we all agreed that this was the last straw. From now on, you are forbidden from leaving the grove. One of us will come with you when you have your playtime, to be sure there's no more tomfoolery afoot. You will stay in the trees, where it's safe."

"Mum, you can't!" He protested.

Even though he couldn't see it, he knew she was raising her brow. "'Can't'? Don't you tell me what I can or can't do. I'll do as I bloody well please."

"No!" Morrel tugged at her apron. "Please, don't. I won't ever go outside again, I promise. I won't talk to the princess or anyone else, just please don't do this."

Her eyes softened. She pulled him into a hug. "Oh, Morrel. I know you want more from this life. The grove's too small for you, just as it was for your grandfather. Believe me when I say I'm doing this because I love you more than anything in the world. You're my boy, and I'd… well, I'd fight a rabbit to stop you from ever getting hurt." She kneeled, so they were both at eye level. She placed her warm, soft hands on his shoulders. "I know it hurts, but believe me when I say this is for your own good."

A lump formed in Morrel's throat. Just like that, all of his dreams of becoming a knight, of exploring the world, were gone. He couldn't argue with her. There *was* no arguing with her. Anytime he wanted to play with Daeyvon and the others from now on, Mum or some other grown-up would be there, making sure they wouldn't wander too far. He would spend the rest of his life here, wishing he could be out there.

Before tears could fully drip onto the floor, he pushed his mum away and ran onto his hammock, curling into a ball and pulling a blanket over his head. Even though it was too warm for a blanket, with the fire and the summer heat, he did it anyway, lying in his makeshift cocoon and wishing he could crawl away into some dark hole. He took deep, shaky breaths, trying not to make his crying too loud. He felt a hand gently shake his shoulder.

"Morrel?" Mum asked. "Did you want some stew?"

He ignored her. Even the delicious meal wouldn't help, and he didn't want anything to do with her right now. Morrel just lay there, crying, his eyes squeezed shut. He heard her eventually move away, going back to whatever she was doing before he came home. She liked to knit together new sheets for the frogs around the grove, and he could hear the wooden needles clanking together. He wished she would be quiet. He wished he could just fall asleep.

Eventually, he got his wish.

Morrel stood in front of a great mountain. It glittered in the sunlight with a hundred different colors, from red, to blue, to green. It was the tallest thing he had ever seen in his life. Bigger than the dandelion trees. Bigger even than Princess Lerelei's tower. It went through the clouds and into the purple sky, maybe even into outer space. Around him, the grass was red, but for once it didn't go over his head. In fact, it went no higher than his ankles.

That was when he realized he was in a suit of armor. Silver, dazzlingly bright armor, fitting his body perfectly. A visor covered his eyes, and strapped to his back, he could feel a sword. When it was in his hands, he could see just how long it was, but he had no problems holding it. Morrel was a knight, through and through. Tall and confident and happy.

"Like it?" Asked Daeyvon, standing next to him.

"Why are you here?" Morrel asked. The question wasn't rude, but rather questioning. His friend was the last person he expected to see in this new place.

Daeyvon shook his head. "I'm not Dae. I just look like him. It's less confusing that way. I don't have much time here, so we can't spend forever asking too many questions."

Morrel nodded. It made total sense to him.

"As to why I'm here," Daeyvon continued, "I'm here to help you. You want to be a knight, right? You want to leave the grove and explore this wondrous world?"

"Yes. More than anything."

Dae smiled. "That's what I thought. So, Lorenna said she'd make you a knight once she was cured, right? Well, if you go to that mountain, you can find it."

"Really?" Morrel asked. It seemed too good to be true.

"Really. It's a long journey, but you can handle it. You can handle anything, Morrel."

The compliment felt real. Genuine. "How do I get there? What is the cure?"

"You'll know it when you see it. Trust me."

A cold wind blew through the grass. Morrel shivered, hugging himself. He could feel it, even through his suit of armor. "Who are you?"

Daeyvon smiled again. His teeth were a spotless white. "I'm a friend. Go north. You'll find the cure on top of the mountain there. I'll be waiting."

When Morrel woke up, he found that his blanket had fallen off in his sleep. It was cold, the fire extinguished, so he hopped to the floor, grabbing the blanket. He wrapped it around him, immediately feeling snugger. His face was raw from crying, but weirdly, he felt good. Taking the blanket off, he rummaged underneath his hammock, grabbing a brown knapsack and stuffing it with the few snacks Mum kept around the house. He took a canteen, filled it with water from the stream outside, and went back in to put it in his bag. Lastly, he opened Grandad's old trunk. Digging through his clothes and trinkets, he found the bottom, where his armor was kept. It was just two round, wooden plates, held together by rope and forming a space where he could stick his head through, so one plate was covering his chest and another his back. It was just that, but Morrel felt like the Rosewood Knight himself.

He looked at Mum. She had fallen asleep on a stump against the wall, her head leaning forward, mouth wide open and snoring. Her knitting needles and half-made sheet lay in her lap. Even in the dark, she looked tired, bags etched underneath her eyes. Left on top of the needles, Morrel's note read:

Dear Mum,

You're right. Our grove is too small for me, but it's not for you. I've gone on an adventure. Please don't come after me.

Love,

Morrel

Morrel hoped she could read his handwriting.

Feeling kind of queasy, he left his home, for the first time ever, not expecting to come back at the end of the day. He hoped Mum wouldn't be too cross. Morrel thought she understood more than anyone why he needed to leave. *It's not like I don't like it here. The shade is nice, and I love Mum, and my friends. But I don't understand how she can be satisfied doing the same thing every single day. I can't just sit down and knit, or farm mushrooms, or pick berries. I want to see the world beyond. What other creatures besides frogs are like. Abyss, what the land looks like on the other side of the horizon.*

He covered his mouth. Mum would wash his mouth out for cursing. It was a good thing she couldn't hear him, but that was something he would never have thought before. What was happening to him?

Morrel puffed out his chest. He was a knight-to-be. He had to act tough, and tough people cursed sometimes.

"Best not make a habit of it, though," he whispered to himself as he journeyed down the dark tunnel. He tread lightly on his feet, anxious not to wake anyone up. The last thing he needed was anyone asking why he was walking around in the middle of the night, without his Mum, and with a knapsack filled with a week's worth of supplies.

That was when it really hit Morrel what he was doing. He kept walking, but he wasn't concentrating on his destination anymore. He kept thinking about Mum waking up and finding his note. He thought about Grandad, who probably also snuck out in the middle of the night. Had he also left a note? A note promising to return to his wife and children? Would Morrel ever come back? He barely wanted to acknowledge his last, selfish, thought, though he spared it half of a second.

When his adventure was over, when he reached the mountain, got the princess's cure, and became her sworn knight, would he even want to come back?

Morrel was outside, now. The grove was dark, and the trees rustled in the wind, but that wasn't what made him afraid. He was afraid of walking away from the only home he had ever known. He was still so young, and he didn't feel ready. He glanced back, to the entrance to the cave. Maybe he would wait a few years. Get taller, learn how to be more grown-up. Except that in a few years, he might not get a chance to leave. He might not get a chance to leave ever again.

He was also afraid of seeing who was in front of him. Afraid of saying goodbye to his best friend.

Daeyvon hopped off the boulder he had picked as a seat. "So, you're really doing it?"

Morrel swallowed. "I am."

Dae sighed. "Listen – I know we always talked about going outside. We even did a few times. Played in the fields around the grove, tried to talk to a few passing marionettes. Maybe our parents are right, though. I mean, it's been fun, but..."

Morrel looked at him. "But what?"

"Maybe it's time to grow up."

Morrel felt stiff. It stung to hear that from Daeyvon. His closest companion through all the years they had known each other. In a way,

Morrel looked up to him. He was tall and strong and confident, and daring, or so Morrel had thought.

He had gone this far. No one could stop him now.

"I'm going," Morrel announced. He tried to make his voice not shake. "I'm going, and when you see me next, I'll be a knight."

He walked past Daeyvon. Daeyvon didn't try to stop him. He walked past the boulders, the pond, and the dandelion trees. He walked past the mossy ground, the stick that he had played with the other day, the place where Cadissa had fallen and broken her arm last year. He stood on the edge of the tree line, his home behind him, Lorenna's tower behind that. He looked out into the night, at the cracked moon shining on the flat, grassy landscape.

This was it. In one step, Morrel would be doing what no frog had ever done since his grandfather. He would be disobeying his mum, leaving his friends, and abandoning all he had ever known. All at the word that a princess would give him a better life. A life filled with danger, heartbreak, peril, and amazing, thrilling adventure.

Taking a deep breath, Morrel stepped forward, the sun rising to his right, and his long shadow smiling at him to his left.

CHAPTER FOUR

The Rosewood Knight awoke that morning with a plan.

He retrieved a volume from a bookcase, the shelves chipped and sagging to one side so the manuscripts inside had a teetering, tense feeling to them. The book he had in his hands was old, the cover receding along the edges as rot ate away at the brown leather. The Rosewood Knight ran a finger along the spine, wiping away a thick layer of dust and uncovering the ornate lettering inscribed on the side: *Cures for Curses of the Known World.* The text groaned open with a stiffness, as if having sat closed for a very, very long time, and judging from the state of the ruin that the knight and his Castellan now inhabited, it likely had.

The pages were yellowed, illustrations showing lots of different creatures known, dead, or unheard of, as well as organs, herbs, and minerals. The ink had begun to fade away, time sucking away from the writing and pictures, though it was still decipherable. He flipped a large, red bookmark to the side, turning the pages with care so as not to rip the thin, almost transparent material. That was where the Castellan found the Rosewood Knight, late into the morning in his quarters, engrossed in the tedious text.

"My lord, may I interest you in breakfast this fine morning? I have prepared deviled rabbit eggs, complete with buttered bread fresh out of the oven."

Though the meal might have seemed appealing to the Rosewood Knight in the past, he did not bother looking up from the book.

"Nay," he said, waving the Castellan away. To his annoyance, the marionette kept jabbering on.

"Will you be paying the Lady Lerelei a visit today?"

"Why is it you need to know?"

"I only inquire so that I may decide on whether to prepare a luncheon."

The Rosewood Knight stood up, backing the Castellan slowly out of the room. He was significantly taller than the servant. "Here is what you need to know: Assume that I will always require a meal. That's your duty, isn't it? To cook for me, clean for me, serve me? If I am not there to eat the slop you call food, you can feed it to the rabbits."

The Castellan bowed. "Please accept my humblest of apologies." He started creeping down the stairs, his lifeless fingers itching the railing as if they were stiff, trying to figure out what life should look like.

Rose put a hand on his shoulder. "Stop."

The Castellan stopped.

"You need not apologize. It is I who should be apologizing to you, old friend. You only mean to help. The Codex dictates that a knight treats his subjects with honor and respect, lest I beseech the gods to strip my armor of honor. If I am not to practice its teachings, day in and day out, who am I for people to call knight? To answer your question, I do not mean to visit the Lady Lerelei today. She is… cross with me. I suppose that is why my demeanor has been less than gentleman-like."

The Codex was the volume of which Rose knew all knights must adhere to, and one he tried to reference often. It would be dishonorable, to say the least, to break its commandments.

The smiling half of the marionette's face seemed to be particularly vibrant. "I understand, Sir. I am certain that, in good time, she shall come to realize you mean only the best for her."

The Rosewood Knight edged into his room. "That is my wish, good Castellan. Yes, I expect I shall stay for luncheon, though I may leave shortly thereafter. I mean to quest upon some ingredients I need."

His servant bowed. "As you wish, my lord."

The marionette kept on murmuring as he wandered down the stairs. Rose shut his door once more and returned to the yellowed texts. *Leech the dragon. Pluck the basilisk… what else? What am I missing?* He scoured the pages as fast as the delicate material would allow him to, being very careful to not let his gloves rip the paper, nor for his sweat to stain the ink. The formula was complex, indeed, but he thought he had cracked the code before the Castellan had interrupted him. *This volume was made for my exact purpose, and yet its answers still find ways to elude me!*

The Rosewood Knight ate a rushed meal of sausages burnt black, paired with sliced potatoes roasted and salted. He washed it all down with a swig from the brown leather flask he kept at his side, and went outside, shield on his back, sword at his belt, and armor gleaming in the mid-day sun. Rose hoped that whichever cooks Lorenna kept in her tower would not burn simple meals into charcoal quite as much as the Castellan did, though his drink helped drown out the taste. When the marionette asked him where he was off to, Rose lied, saying he needed a breath of fresh air. *I do not need any more of his pestering. He actually presumes far too much for a marionette. There's a reason his old lord left him in these ruins, all alone. I told him I was leaving, and that is all he needs to know.*

As he rode, the Rosewood Knight wondered whether the marionette would have enough direction to do the daily chores on his own, but dismissed the idea. It wasn't right of him to think so little of his faithful servant. He half expected Windsoar to emit a huff as if in agreement of his unchivalrous behavior, but the steed remained silent, as usual. For that, the Rosewood Knight was glad.

It had been a few hours since Rose left his keep. It was now the late evening, and the air felt thick with mist. It had rolled in across the moors, an unusual sight for the lonely Heartlands, but not entirely unheard of. *If it allows me opportune time to slay this beast, then so be it.* He was approaching a grove of trees, and so was the first ingredient he needed.

The trees were silent, the usual buzzing of insects and forest creatures gone. Whether they were slumbering, silent, or nonexistent, Rose didn't care. He cursed at the fact that they were gone, since it would be much harder to hide his presence to his prey. For what he hunted was no scared deer or aurox. It was a basilisk. A creature that only with a slight touch from its feathers, could petrify any living thing. And now, as the Rosewood Knight gazed at the grove of trees, he was sure that it wasn't asleep. The leaves, blown forward by a gust of wind who knew how long ago, were now in stasis. They extended on the branches, and, in the case of the smaller branches, the branches themselves, in such a way that was impossible for a natural forest phenomenon to pull off. If it wasn't frozen by the basilisk's touch, then it would have fallen back into place, gazing at the forest floor below.

It had been difficult to track down the beast's lair. The locals had proven useless, pointing him in vague directions in the mannerisms that seemed normalized within the marionette society. Rose's castellan seemed to be the most talkative of their bunch, judging by the way the traveling groups would only gesture and use weird signals, rather than choosing speech. The Rosewood Knight found himself almost wondering if they were capable of the ability at all, if not for the existence of the Castellan and the fact that they gasped and murmured when they laid lifeless eyes upon Windsoar to prove otherwise.

To his annoyance, he had stumbled upon the frozen forest by pure accident. Rose had been following a small creek, its waters babbling upon small stones and curves in its path across the land. Flowers lined the creek, comprising about thirty petals each, the tips of which started as a pleasant, sunset orange, then slowly deepened into a dark shade of purple as they neared the center. The petals were strange, as well, almost resembling human ears as their bodies thinned until they reached the center of the head. The centers were covered in the pollen that allowed them to spread all the way down the creek, though they moved about curiously. The taller of the plants reached his height as he rode Windsoar, and so once he plucked the head of a flower off its green stem. The pollen seeds erupted from the center, buzzing about his helm like insects until he swatted them away, dropping the plucked flower to drift away downstream.

The creek had once been part of a great river, that was clear enough. The banks were long since dried, now home to the beds of flowers as they brushed the gurgling, clear shadow of its former self. The occasional dandelion tree grew along the shore, briefly giving the Rosewood Knight some nice shade from the glaring sun overhead. He knew it did not bother Windsoar. Assuming his mount was capable of feeling heat, his molten center would surely have given him taste enough, and Rose was riding him through the stream, if that offered any cooling to the statzel-modeled marionette. The grasses above the ridge that formed from the riverbank were a combination of deep red and vibrant emerald, spanning flat land save for the rare lump of a hill or tight grove of trees, sometimes disrupted by brush and general vegetation.

So, there the Rosewood Knight was, standing before a grove of trees. He remembered a quote by one of the writers of *Cures for Curses*: *Yet while the land around breathed, they held their breath, for this was the domain of a beast most foul.*

Dismounting Windsoar, he winced at the sound of his boots against the ground. He reminded himself that it would be difficult to catch the basilisk by surprise. Rose ventured deeper into the grove, drawing his sword to hack away at the thick foliage that blocked his way forward. Yet when the blade met the branches and leaves, it bounced off the surface with a *thunk!* Rose stared. The sword had left a cut, to be sure, but it was tiny compared to what it should have done. Instead of crashing to the side as he plowed through the infernal overgrown forest, the plants remained upright, as if they were massive trees.

Very well, Rose thought. *Wood can be cut down.* Muscles straining, he lifted the weapon, the point zooming through the stale air, then brought it swinging into the bushes. With a snap, the many tangled branches fell apart, smoking rising from the red-hot wake that the Rosewood Knight left. The smell of sweat and metal filling his nostrils, he hacked his way through the forest, gritting his teeth at every sound of destruction that exploded in the quiet forest, and very likely, the beast's own sharp ears.

The grove was not very large. At least, it had not looked it as he had approached the trees before. Rose estimated that it would not take long before he would find the bloody creature. Yet, as he cleared the woods piece by piece, he could still not find it. *It is a good thing Lorenna is not here to see me now, looking under every rock and twig, like a child at play. How she would laugh and laugh.* Feeling a sudden rush of fury, the Rosewood Knight swung his sword at the base of a tree. It was not the largest dandelion he had ever come across, maybe as wide as him, with some added forgiveness on the said measurement. Yet one swing was not enough. The blade stuck in the tree, carving a smile that bit onto the blade and held, until Rose tore it out through its pursed lips. Again, Rose struck, sending bits of sawdust into the air. Sweat was beginning to drip inside of his hot, metal armor, making him feel as if he needed to rip it off his body and be rid of it for good. Instead, he swung the sword again.

And again.

And again.

The third time, the tree fell.

The dandelion crashed to the forest floor. It scattered brush and their fallen leaves, though the leaves did not float into the air so much as splinter through it. He grunted as one bounced off his armor, sending the ringing noise of metal into the air. Staring at the ground, Rose saw that the leaf had split in two at his feet, presumably from the impact of the collision. Slowly, he crouched down and picked up a half of the material, examining its many veins that ran throughout the green surface. The inside, which was now visible because of the break, was oozing juices, as if it was just the surface of the leaf that had been petrified.

With a start, he realized that the forest was no longer still. The leaves were shifting, at first as if they were merely caught in an odd breeze, but he knew that was impossible. No, something underneath was moving them upwards. Slowly and with great effort, with the weight that a stone mason would lift piles of bricks above his shoulders. The Rosewood Knight watched as the basilisk lifted its head from underneath the leaf pile.

It looked nothing like how it was illustrated in his book. That illustration had been of a creature that looked like the common poultry, but with a curled, scaled tail, short, leathery wings, and a largely feathered neck. A mouth with a yellow beak full of pointed fangs. It seemed as if the scholars who had contributed to the volume had been very, very wrong. This thing before him was a mass of thin flesh, bones poking through its skin, in odd and disjointed places where one would think bones shouldn't even be. A dull pink waddle dangled from underneath its beak. Yellow eyes with black pupils that were so dilated they nearly overtook the entire space blinked slowly, and not in unison. Gray feathers hung off its sagging flesh, brushing onto the ground and waving with every step, as if determined to spread its venom to everything it could lay its greasy wings on. A long, naked, pink tail whipped back and forth in the air. Though it was shorter than the Rosewood Knight, it was still far greater than any bird he was accustomed to, as it slowly stood on its legs and stared at him squarely in the helm. The basilisk looked like the state that Rose feared he would find it in: just having woken up.

It extended its wings, intimidatingly covering Rose in its shadow, and raised its talons. They were sharp, cruel things, cracked and jagged. The tail dangled below it as it rose into the air, swishing back and forth. The worst of the basilisk, however, was the sound. It began as a sort of croak, a fermented noise at the back of its throat that the basilisk opened its beast to hack out. Once it met the air, however, it turned from a croak, to a wet belch, to an earth-shaking, high-pitched scream. Screams only came across naturally in the dead of night, when someone was walking through long forgotten ruins or an abandoned lichyard. They would cause one's mount to rear, nearly knocking its rider off, or, at best, the lantern held in hand. Later, after running in terror, or for those braver, clutching their sword as they scanned their immediate vicinity, they would laugh at themselves. It was the sound of a mountain cat, emitting queer sounds as a part of their mating practices. A creepy phenomenon, but one that could be easily explained. This was not. This was unlike anything the Rosewood Knight had ever come across.

"What VVitchery is this?" Rose spat as he squared himself. He held his sword in both hands, favoring a sturdier weapon rather than duel wielding that and the shield which he kept on Windsoar. That, however, clearly had its downsides, as the basilisk launched itself at him, scraping its nails against his breastplate and gnashing pointed teeth at his head. The beast was much, much faster than Rose could have anticipated. In that moment, he was very grateful for his decision to keep his armor on, otherwise he would have definitely been petrified by the basilisk's feathers.

The impact of the initial attack knocked him off his sturdy stance, sending him onto the ground. The hard, rock-like surface of the foliage caused his armor to clatter painfully against his spine. He eyed the basilisk's beak from behind his visor. This was a monster that petrified its prey in order to slow their movement and devour them easier. In order to consume the hard surface, it would need a powerful, bone-breaking beak. This was something Rose became painfully aware of as it lunged at him, snapping at the gaps between his armor, including the slits in his visor. Not only did teeth line the inside of its beak, but its purple tongue also bristled with sharp, needle-like bone.

Rose pushed the basilisk off his breastplate, careful to touch it only with his gauntlets, and even still trying his best to avoid the feathers. He rolled over, landing in a crouched position, sword in hand. He used his grounded position to boost himself forward, attempting a jab at the beast. He could see the sunlight glinting off its metal as *Last One* pointed straight between its eyes. However, the Rosewood Knight had forgotten about his surroundings. Namely, the petrification that the bushes, leaves, and grass had experienced. His boots caught on a jagged piece of brush, and he fell face-forward, dropping his sword and using his arms to shield himself from the main force of the impact.

The Rosewood Knight felt talons scraping against his helmet, and almost too late did he realize what the basilisk was doing. It was grabbing at the ridges of the helm and the gaps in the visor, attempting to lift off the armor from his head. It was already rising, the bottom of the helm almost reaching his chin. Thankfully, he wore a layer of clothing underneath, covering his back well enough so that the feathers did not brush against bare skin. With both hands, he grabbed at his helmet, wrestling it away from the basilisk's thin legs. As he grabbed hold, he slammed it into the vermin's body, briefly forcing it away from him so that he could put back on his headwear.

He edged away from the creature as it spun in the air, reorienting itself. *I cannot get close enough to it, since it'll remove my armor. I cannot use brute force, because it has made a treacherous terrain for its home. I have no crossbow or sling, so I cannot use longer distances to my advantage. Blast it, it has me trapped. I was foolish to stumble into its lair so carelessly.* He dashed behind a tree, avoiding the more deadly petrified bits of vegetation below him. Rose could hear the creature's breathing from the other side of the tree. It was clawing at the hard bark, climbing it with sharp nails. The basilisk's inhales were like that of an old man, clawing at his last seconds of life before the veil would take him forever.

That's what they all do in the end, isn't it? Exhale their defeat. What point is there in fighting something the likes of which you have no hope of beating, for in that moment, it knows more than you, is stronger than you, and hungers for you. At that moment, the Rosewood Knight thought of Lorenna, awaiting him in her tower. A torch in the night, and a beacon in the day. He thought of how he might never lay eyes on the flag, rippling in the breeze, as it tugged at her hair and rich silks draped around her figure.

Then it came to him. *Accepting defeat. Accepting death. It is for those who are ready to die. I am not.*

Slowly, he edged from out of his hiding place. Retrieving his weapon, Rose scanned the area for any sign of the basilisk. He had heard it, mere moments before. It was ridiculous to assume that it had given up.

Oh no, this was food that had wandered into its very den. This was too good of an opportunity for this beast to pass up. It was not hiding, no. It was waiting.

His guess proved true. From out of the canopies, it leapt. Rose only had time to see its descending shadow before the basilisk was upon him. He took a step backward and swiped his sword up, creating a line of red across the beast's underbelly. It roared again. Rose saw the blood drip onto the ground. *I may have scratched it, but this is not the right place for the killing. It's going to be angry at me, now, and a beast cornered, especially in its home, is far more dangerous than I dare imagine.*

In a blur, the basilisk dove at him. Again, instead of running, Rose side-stepped the attack. He was backing away now, in the closest direction to the plains outside, he hoped. The creature was running on the ground now, using its legs to gain ground on him rather than using the air. It was a fast learner, and that was something Rose didn't like. He swung at it with his sword as he kept backing away. Once, he spared a split second to look behind him to check for obstacles, and that was when the basilisk struck.

It jumped, landing its large body on his forearm. It dug its talons into the space between his pieces of armor, splitting his flesh, curved nails making uneven cuts, going deeper and deeper. The basilisk was too close now for Rose to effectively use his blade, and so he had no choice but to thrash his arm and punch and claw at the monster to get it off of him. It was pecking at other vulnerable parts of his body, turning his armor an ever-deeper shade of red. The basilisk was eating him, piece by piece.

Rose grabbed it by the leg, using the limb as a hold to whip the creature. In his grip, he felt the beast's bones cracking, and his action was confirmed by yet another scream from the sorry monster. The Rosewood Knight threw it onto the ground, as it yelped and flapped its wing, limping as the injured leg dribbled blood onto the ground. Now was his chance. Rose dashed towards the edge of the grove, ignoring the searing pain all throughout his chest and forearms. He was made slower by the weight of the steel upon his body, but it didn't matter. The basilisk would not catch up in time.

He reached the edge of the clearing, breaking petrified leaves as he broke from the brush. The sun was more dominant out here, and so he had only to look at the shadows to see when to dive to the ground. It was just in time, too, as the basilisk passed him overhead, its talons extended and wings flapping. It was leaving a stream of blood through the air, and it clearly had been too much, as its eyes grew tired and it crashed onto the grass.

The Rosewood Knight stood, panting, watching it flail about. Its feathers were brushing every living thing around it, trapping itself in shards of grass and daisies. He calmly walked over to Windsoar, who had been waiting patiently for its master to finish his business. Rose retrieved his satchel, and stood over the basilisk. It was getting pierced by the blades of grass as it attempted to escape the trap of its own making. Rose stooped, and plucked a feather from its back. He stored it into his satchel, and retrieved his flask in the process.

The basilisk was wailing. A terrible, irritable wailing, as even more shards of grass impaled its flesh. *It was wise to make a domain for itself,* the Rosewood Knight thought. *It was not wise to venture out of it. Its vile, VVitch powers were its own undoing, and now, here I stand over it. Victorious.*

This encounter had only made the Rosewood Knight more determined to finish his quest. Nothing would stand in his way. Not even death.

He grabbed the flask. It had been exposed to the sun as he had been fighting the basilisk. Partially lifting his helm, the hot liquid met his lips, and he grimaced.

CHAPTER FIVE

Morrel the marsh frog had finally done it. He had stepped outside. Beyond.

And he couldn't be happier. No, he most definitely could not. The tallgrass went just over his head, making it hard to see where he was going unless he jumped up. While that was fun, Morrel was all too aware that bouncing up and down would attract unwanted attention. Namely, of the rabbit variety.

They looked adorable with their coats of black, white, gray, and brown, but that was just to catch their prey unawares. They were vicious meat eaters, using yellow, pointed teeth to hunt anything that moved across the Heartlands. Between them, news of a basilisk that had made a home for itself not too far away, and the most terrible of them all, the horse flies, the Heartlands was a vicious, unforgiving place. Morrel could not get enough of it.

Everywhere he looked, he wanted to explore. The small anthill next to the reeds, where purple workers clicked their mouths, looking for food. A cloud of pink butterflies flew from the south, tickling Morrel's cheeks, making him giggle, before they flew off to nest somewhere else. He ran, not being able to help himself. The food inside of his knapsack jiggled as he ran, but he was sure they'd be fine. They were mostly ginger snaps, so at worst they'd crumble, and Morrel was a daring adventurer, not afraid to scoop the crumbs from the bag and eat them like that. He ran and ran, wanting to get as deep inside of the world as he possibly could. Now that he was away from home, *really* away, it felt like he had an amazing amount of freedom.

"Why, I could eat cookies until I burst!" He proclaimed, panting as he continued to sprint. "I could look at the sun without adults telling me not to. Ow." Rubbing his eye, he slowed. "Okay, I must remember to channel the wisdom of a knight, too. Princess Lorenna will *not* be impressed if I blind myself. Ooh!"

His train of thought broke as he scooped up something from the ground, quick as a fox. Opening up his palms, he gently let the head of a mouse peek out from between his green fingers. It squeaked, trying to squirm out of its new cage.

"Oh, sorry, mousy! Don't worry, I'm not going to eat you or anything like that. I've never been able to catch one of you before. Once I came close, when Mum found one in the kitchen. She wouldn't let me pick it up when I cornered it, though. We trapped it in a pot and moved it outside, instead. I had to scrub the pot after that, too. Can you believe it?" He laid his hand gently onto the ground. "Here you go. I'm your friend, see? No need to be frightened."

Opening his hands, the mouse darted out, practically a blur as it scurried away from Morrel. He stumbled back. "Whoa! Where are you off to in such a hurry?"

Checking the sky for birds of prey, he started following the mouse's tiny pawprints in the dirt once he confirmed there was none. Whatever it was scared of, it wasn't up above, and so Morrel thought he better follow it, in case he needed shelter from something in the area. It would've come as quite a shock to everyone around him, but Morrel was not very good with a blade. He hadn't had anything good to practice with, save a sharpened stick and a kitchen knife, until Mum had taken that away. If it came down to avoiding the predator and having to fight it, Morrel thought that some of his wisdom he was trying to channel said it was better to avoid it.

The mouse prints wove between reed and grass, until they stopped at… his eyes widened. Mushrooms! A whole circle of them! Blue stems with plump, red caps, spotted in white. Forgetting about the mouse, Morrel's mouth drooled. He slowly approached the circle, licking his lips. He could make himself a nice stew. He thought it seemed pretty easy. Morrel had seen Mum do it a million times. Or he'd just eat them as they were. He reached for one, plucking it from the ground. It was light as a feather, and the smell was rich and earthy, with just a hint of something like vanilla.

He began to plop it into his mouth, when Morrel paused, remembering something. Tongue hanging out, he thought back to something Granddad had told him, when he was very little. Something about mushrooms with red caps…

He threw the fungus to the ground, stomping on it for good riddance. It probably would've tasted delicious, and then he'd clutch his chest and fall to the ground, dead. It was poisonous. Venomous? Morrel could never remember the difference. Grandad had spent countless hours exploring nature, so if anyone knew about which mushrooms to avoid, it was him. Shame, though. Now he wanted mushrooms.

The ground in front of him moved, bits of soil and pebbles tumbling to his feet. Looking, Morrel prepared to chew the mouse out for leading him to potentially get killed. It was not the mouse that he saw.

At first, it looked like thick, brown roots growing from the ground. They formed a sort of cross, each point ending in round knobs. Then, Morrel spotted the glint of metal at their base, and he realized what it was. Arms burning, he pulled and pulled, until the sword was freed from the earth.

It was an old thing. A silver blade held together by twisting roots from some plant or tree Morrel didn't recognize. It was long, almost too long for him to carry, but when Morrel held it, it felt right in his hands. The handle perfectly fit the curve of his fingers, roots twisting around them in natural harmony.

Dropping the weapon, Morrel threw himself to the ground as he felt the ground begin to shake. It wasn't an earthquake. It was a horse galloping towards them. He knew from experience that he should drop and roll out of the way in these types of instances. Cadissa had nearly gotten herself trampled by the knight from the Midnight Sea in the past, since she and every other marsh frog were too short for human folk to see them while riding. Today, though, it was not Haera who rode past Morrel, trampling grass and mushroom in their wake. It was a knight clad in red and silver, atop a statzel made of bronze gears and twisted metal. It was the Rosewood Knight who went past, unsurprisingly not seeing Morrel. It was Morrel who saw the new sword shift so that it was pointing to Rose's own weapon, hanging at his side. Grabbing the handle, the marsh frog felt the blade tug, as if wanting to fly towards the knight's sword.

Digging his feet into the ground, Morrel huffed as the pull grew stronger, like it was desperate to catch the knight before he could get too far away. It dragged Morrel, dust rising as his heels dug deeper into the soil.

Reaching a firm rock, Morrel managed to hold his ground, panting. His first act as a knight-to-be would not be skewering the princess's warrior.

Several tense moments later, the pull released, and he dropped the sword to rest on the ground. He stared at the strange weapon. It wasn't like Rose's, with alien circles etched into the metal, or like Haera's, whose own blade was a simple longsword made of plain steel. This was older. Felt… different.

Hearing a squeak, he turned his head. Underneath a mushroom, the mouse cowered, body trembling. A foul smell rose through the air, and at first Morrel thought the little creature had gotten *very* scared, until he realized it came from where the Rosewood Knight went off to. He must have squashed some creature by accident. The marionette of his was so fast he probably didn't even realize when things like that happened.

"Hey," Morrel said, crawling forward. "I already told you, I'm not going to hurt you. C'mon, what are you so afraid of? Is it the sword?" He hefted it up, admiring how the sun glinted off the surface.

It was not, he found out, the sword. A low growl came from the brush behind him, and he remembered that the mouse had never been running away from him. It had been running away from something else, and as Morrel turned around, he was face-to-face with the predator.

The rabbit bared its teeth, cracked from chewing through bone, sharp from years of doing it. Its eyes weren't the soft brown of the mouse's, but too dark to be any sort of color. Dark, and hungry. Its long ears were pulled back as it prowled Morrel, paws leaving sharp tracks in the ground. Its fur was black and white, not smooth like a cat's, but ruffled and sharp looking. A wild animal's fur. It was almost as big as a horse, just short enough to hide in the tallgrass, and just quiet enough to pounce on unsuspecting prey. Which it was just about to do.

Once, when Morrel was little, Grandad had read him a bedtime story.

It was a quiet night, just like the night Morrel had left the grove. Mum was over at one of her friend's houses, having a cup of sweet wine as she liked to do from time-to-time. This left Grandad in charge of Morrel. Morrel thought this was unfair, because he was perfectly capable of taking care of himself, and it was more fun to have the whole house to himself. It wasn't up to him, though, even after he voiced his complaints, so Grandad came over, with a large, leather book in his hands.

He put on a pot of stew, but it was far worse than when Mum made it. Morrel did his best to pretend to enjoy it as he bounced on his lap, waiting for him to finally put on his spectacles and open the book. Morrel liked this book, because it had lots of pictures, and lots of stories. They had only read through a few of them before, and he was certain that Grandad would read him a new story tonight. Indeed, he did.

Grandad cleared his throat. "Once upon a time, not so very long ago, there was a mighty warrior from the evermeadow. This warrior was famous among their people as a knight who slayed monsters. Every time the jarl needed one of these terrifying monsters defeated, this knight was the one for the job." He flipped to the next page. It showed a picture of the knight, tall and with green armor. "One day, the jarl summoned the knight to his chambers. He said there was a monster up in the mountains, hunting the folk that lived up there. It was very deadly, and the soldiers he had sent never returned. This was why the jarl needed the knight."

"Now, the knight had been doing this for some years now. As they saw it, the jarl sent them time after time to risk their life, and never gave them anything in return. The knight was not greedy, so they did not ask for treasure or land. They whispered into the jarl's ear what they wanted. What they wanted was what the jarl loved dearly. What they wanted…"

Grandad paused, frowning and squinting at the paper. Morrel stirred. "Is there something wrong?"

He looked up, "Hmm? Oh, no, no, not at all. It's just… I don't like this part, that's all. I'll skip to the good stuff."

Morrel just shrugged and went back to staring at the fire. "The jarl agreed to give the knight their desire. After that, the warrior set out on their quest." The next drawing showed the knight riding on their horse, towards colorful mountains in the distance. "Over stump and stone, river and ramble, they made their way to the mountains. It did not take them long to find where the monster was hiding. The village had been burned to the ground, and all the marionettes had left. So when something moved behind a wooden house, the knight knew it was what they were hunting."

Morrel gasped. Grandad looked at him. "Do you want me to stop? Is it too scary?"

He shook his head. "No, no. Keep going." Morrel would be brave.

"Very well." The next picture was of a man in shadow, with details barely visible. "The knight prepared to vanquish this foul foe, but before they even drew their sword, something caused them to stop. This monster did not look like a monster at all. It looked like a man. So the knight asked this man if they had done this."

"'Yes,' replied the man. 'However, 'tis not of mine own will that I would cause this carnage. 'Tis the work of a VVitch, who put thine truly under a spell. Now that I have done their Abyssal work, I am free, but not free of mine shame.'"

"The man closed his eyes, waiting for the knight to end them for hurting so many people. Instead, he felt their hand on his shoulder, and he knew that he was forgiven. 'Together,' the knight said, 'We shall slay this vile VVitch.'"

Grandad closed the book. "The knight realized that the monster was not really his enemy at all. The monster was just as scared as the people around him."

The rabbit growled at Morrel again. Steadying his shaking hands, Morrel slowly lowered the sword to the ground, raising his hands as he stood straight. "I'm your friend. Look, I didn't hurt that mouse. I won't hurt you. Even if… I look like lunch…" It snarled. Heart racing, Morrel began to walk forward, walking closer to the creature. *Grandad, your stories better be worth something.* "I'm going to the mountains, up north. Do you wanna come with me? I'm not very heavy, I could ride on your back."

The creature's eyes shifted to the sword lying on the ground. "I'm not going to hurt you," Morrel reassured it once again. Slowly, he reached out, touching it on the snout. He tried not to flinch as the rabbit tensed. Instead, Morrel kept petting it, letting out soft coos. The rabbit's mouth stopped baring its teeth, and miraculously, it relaxed, rolling on the ground, awaiting a belly scratch.

Morrel laughed. "You're not so bad, are you?"

After many minutes of appeasing the big softie, Morrel climbed onto its back. It wasn't soft, exactly, but not nearly as harsh as it had seemed when he thought he was about to be eaten. Scratching it behind the ear, he declared: "I think I'll name you… Deborah!"

Deborah seemed to like that. It pounded the ground with its back leg, a long, pink tongue lolling out of its mouth.

"Wanna go on my adventure? Let's gOOooo–!" Morrel's sentence broke as the rabbit began to run. He had just enough time to stoop down and grab his new sword before they were off, hopping across the sea of red grass. He clung onto the rabbit's hair, hoping pulling on it too much wouldn't irritate his friend. Up above, he felt as invincible as the Rosewood Knight. They were heading to the mountains, and there, Morrel would finish his quest.

Not until later did he notice the long, thin cut that the sword had accidentally left as he dragged it with him. The blood was the same color as the grass, and it left a long stain across his clothes. Looking at his reflection in the metal, it was red and distorted.

CHAPTER SIX

Riding back to the tower of his future betrothed, the Rosewood Knight recollected what he had read in his book.

Before finding the basilisk, he had combed through the parchments, eventually stumbling on one that had provided a solution. A piece to his puzzle. "A dragon's blood holds many intriguing properties," Rose read. He felt it helped get the words across if he read the text aloud. "It is pondered by many scholars of the fourteenth year of Dim Light that the substance known as leukocyte may aid in the process of transmitting its own infectious curses. It is thought, by some, that the leukocyte prevents its own body from falling victim to the illness, whilst simultaneously aiding the dragon in spreading it to others, particularly humans, who of all species in the animal kingdom, evade its roaring flames the easiest, though perhaps airborne curses not so much." The first time the Rosewood Knight had read the section, his heart had leapt for relief, thinking that the dragon's blood was the only ingredient he required.

"It should be noted that, however pleasing the thought of obtaining leukocyte might be, it grows foul upon exit of the bloodstream. To cure a curse using dragon's blood, preventing them from falling ill to the same affliction ever again, the leecher would also need an item, whether that be of man or of natural flesh, that prevented the blood from reacting to the outside air. Something which, through numerous trials, has been found not to work with a simple vial." That was when Rose thought of the basilisk, and the first step in his quest had ensued.

Once I drive my blade through the belly of the dragon, I can use the feather to freeze a droplet of blood. One drop should be enough, but once I bring it to the Lady Lerelei to consume, how shall I de-petrify the blood? She will not be cured of her curse if the blood is frozen. Not even the heat of my sword would make the blood run freely down its edge. Why, I would need… something greater.

He flipped to one last page. "There is perhaps no hex, magyk, nor charm more powerful than force of will. Those with minds of steel are often most clad in it as well." He ran a finger along black ink lines, forming the drawing of a warrior in gray armor, sharp, needle-like spikes covering him from head to toe. "Those with the most courageous of hearts carry the most power. Not just in the word of the poet, but also in the literal sense. Very few experiments have been practiced involving the use of the organ, but it has been pondered that if one were to grind the heart into a fine powder, it would be the atlas for many wondrous cures."

Now, the Rosewood Knight rode back to the spire of Lorenna Lerelei. The feather was retrieved, and a dragon was yet to be slain. The third ingredient was a mystery, but one he would no doubt solve. Nothing would get between Rose and his bride-to-be.

The ride between his keep and the tower of Lerelei, while a long one, had grown to be a mundane task. Once he had reached his abode, rather than stopping, he continued onward, riding with the sun on a new day. He passed his dog kennels, located near the keep. A square, gray ruin with a spiked fence built around it. The Castellan fed his hounds regularly. They had tried to maul the marionette, once, but relented once they could not find the taste of living flesh.

The events of the night before had left him tired, muscles aching and wounds hissing from his battle with the basilisk. However, he put aside the discomfort, and rode onwards. The motion of Windsoar underneath his armor. The light reflecting off the golden and silver metal. The wind cooling him off. He was still diligent, however. His last encounter with the wild rabbits had not gone well. Today, though, was the usual routine. No creatures of the Heartlands troubled him, and Rose took it as a good omen.

There it was. The tower occupying the flatness, shielded by a small grove of trees. *I should ask if Lorenna is willing to tear them down. It irks me to travel around them every time I arrive.* The closer he got to her home, the louder her laughs became. They sounded joyous, happier than he had ever heard her. His spirits lifted, thinking that she was in the right mood to forgive him.

Vines with white flower petals had bloomed on her balcony overnight, forming a partial tree that he saw her plucking from. She had a ring of them around her head, so thick and in such quantity that it looked more like an elegant crown than a simple circlet. They were a brilliant white, shaded with soft pinks and blues. He noted how the loosely adjusted flowers floated from Lorenna, like a stream of butterflies enveloping her in their vulnerability. The flag of her house still stood tall. Shorter, cruelly shorter, than most castles or keep would display their banners, but still too far away for his metal hands to reach. The white balcony glittered in the warm sunlight. Thousands of tiny stones embedded in the larger marble created a maze of mirrors reflecting light off its surface. Her tower, indeed, seemed like a beacon for her ancient gods.

Rose cleared his throat, assuming his familiar position of a knee to the dirt. His head looked to Lady Lorenna and the vibrant sky beyond. "My lady, my lady, my magnificent Lady of Lerelei! I kneel before you now, begging the question: does thou seek retribution, or embrace forgiveness? It is well known that a rose cannot go for long without a hand being pricked by its thorns, but one does not curse the rose, if one is kind. They curse the planet for blooming a flower so sweet with a twist so sour. Now, I am come before you, in all of my humbleness and sins laid bare."

Lorenna stood, looking over the railing. Her eyes widened, and she did a quick glance into her chambers, before uttering: "Oh–!"

The Rosewood Knight's gaze drifted to her doorway. The curtain of vines, which usually stood between his vision of her chambers and the elevated terrace, was parted. He stood, throwing away all pretenses of noble courtesy. The countless customs and rules to high royalty astounded him when he first looked to the Codex to instruct him in the art. He didn't understand the point of choosing the correct utensil for a meal, the proper way to address a lady, nor even the appropriate posture that a knight was expected to maintain at all costs, or else he shame the name of his house. Yet, Rose participated. He trained his back to arch in a straight line, despite the heavy armor pressing down on his shoulders. He learned to identify which of the dozens of forks, spoons, and knives to use in the context of a feast or supper party. Most importantly, he practiced the art of addressing a lady. He knew to bow, to kiss the delicate hand, to be especially generous with gifts, and to bend the knee.

Damn it all, was all the Rosewood Knight thought when he saw who parted the curtain of Lerelei's flowers.

Haera did not look as she did the night of VVitch's slaying. A smile took over her face. A nightgown covered her flesh. Her hair was disheveled. It was utterly, hopelessly clear, that she had just gotten out of Lorenna's bed. Perhaps this would have been the chance for the Rosewood Knight to have gotten a peek into the princess's chambers, as his curiosity often rubbed away at him, but he did not think to look. In fact, he was not looking at all. All he saw was Haera's smile. *You did not smile when you ran, Selkie. You ran from the tempest. From the gaze and power and embrace of your heathen god. Does your dishonored lover know that, I wonder?*

Haera yawned, stretched, and tied her robe shut. She saw him, Rose knew, but it did not appear to matter to her. It was clear to him that she was used to the attention. Lorenna wasn't moving, apparently fearing what was to come. Haera kissed her head, and joined her on the balcony, overlooking Rose.

Lady Haera spread her arms. "I'm alive."

With a jolt, the Rosewood Knight realized he had reached for the handle of his weapon. He brought the gauntlet to his side. *Straight posture.* "So my eyes tell me. I see also that thou has ravaged the Lady Lorenna's honor, as well." The last words came out in a harsh spit.

Lorenna laid a hand on Haera, as her lover bristled. "Please, I implore you to understand. Living alone in this tower, for so many years, with no one – I have grown lonely. Imagine how overcome with joy I was to discover that my dearest Haera had survived thy terrifying ordeal with VVitch. My Rose –"

The Rosewood Knight swiped at the air, as if slapping away her extended hand. "I am not *thine.* That is clear enough to me, now. I am not thy Rose whose petals you would pluck so idly. Have I not given my flesh, my blood, to climb your spire so dire? Have I not showered you with all that I could give, from the ground? All I wanted was to be thy loving lord husband, and your- your *succubus* has squandered it."

It was now Haera who spoke. "You have done that yourself, vagabond. You act the little lordling, playing castle with thy abandoned keep, but I know who you really are. Did I not tell you on the eve of VVitch's slaying, that I saw through thy flowery armor? You are nothing more than a fly buzzing in Lorenna's ear. Nothing more than a wolf hoping to scale the tree. You are a *pest,* Rose. Now, before I squash you, I encourage you to leave us. Begone."

"Haera," Lerelei began. "Mayhaps you push him too far. After all, his only true crime is his affection for me. Does that deserve such slander?"

Haera looked over at her, surprised. Before she could say anything else, the Rosewood Knight interrupted. "Indeed, my lady. Whilst she kept you company, I was ensuring thy future. The first ingredient I have gathered. The feather of a basilisk. The first ingredient in curing thy affliction which keeps you imprisoned. I have found the way to free you, my lady, and I intend to pursue it." Lorenna put a hand to her mouth, and Rose drew his weapon. Haera tensed. Pointing it at Lorenna's companion, he said: "You have committed sin, Lady Haera. You are craven and unfit for a title of knight. I see an opportunity here, for the both of us. Lorenna, thy honor remains intact, albeit blushed. I hereby challenge Lady Haera to a duel for Lorenna Lerelei's hand in matrimony. Should she win, she can lay safe claim to her honor and do with you as she wishes. Should I, I may merge my house with yours, and a union between Lord and Lady shall be struck." He looked at Haera. *Back down. Prove your worthlessness.* "Do you accept these terms?"

Haera looked over at Lorenna. The princess pursed her lips, then nodded, cheeks flushed. Rose swore that he could hear the Selkie's teeth grinding from where he stood. "I accept, Rosewood Knight." Her fingernails dug at the hard railing.

Though they could not see, Rose was smiling. "I pray our fight is more fearsome than thine with vile VVitch. I am afraid it will not be for at least a fortnight. I must quest upon the final two items of which I need for the cure. Consider this my wedding present to you, Lady Lerelei." The taste of victory was a small, fleeting one, yet it had come, and Rose knew a banquet was on its way.

Lorenna Lerelei watched the Rosewood Knight ride away.

A cure! Could it be true? Might I finally be free of this wretched curse? She could scarcely believe it. For most of her life, this was the only place she had ever known. She had tried so many times to leave – jumping from the balcony, climbing through a window, even lying awake the whole night to await whoever brought her breakfast in the morning. All of them had been to no avail. It was impossible, unthinkable that Rose could gift her freedom from the tower, yet she believed him. As improbable as it seemed, for Lorenna, freedom seemed to have appeared on the horizon.

Despite herself, she smiled broadly. Lorenna took Haera's hands in her own. Her happiness wavered when she felt the hands trembling. She felt guilty. At that moment, she had completely forgotten about the duel. "My dearest Haera, whatever is the matter? I am sure you needn't go through with the agreement, if it is not to thy liking."

Haera closed her eyes, pulling away from Lorenna. Her back was turned. Lorenna could see the outline of her spine as she leaned forward. "I am sworn to you, my lady. I shall never feed you lies. Never."

Lorenna started to reach out, to feel her warmth once again, yet she stopped herself. "Tell me, Haera."

"The last day with you was the greatest I have ever had. I thought, I assumed, you had felt the same way. Then you said nothing, stood by, giving me your blessing as I made this accursed deal with the Rosewood Knight, and now I do not know what I think. Will you truly respect the terms of this duel? It is not a thing so easily broken. If I should fall in battle, will you go to Rose? When you make love to him, will you think of me, or will you be glad to be ridden of your… what? Your friend? Your knight? Your whore?"

Lorenna was trembling, now. "You speak so assuredly. Are you certain that you will fall to his blade? Mayhaps I can plead with him, should that terrible destiny come to pass. He loves me, mayhaps he will spare your life. Mayhaps –"

Haera whirled around, now facing Lorenna. "Mayhaps and methinks. This and that. As I said, all I know is the truth. The truth is that I ran when battle called me to defeat VVitch. Yet, the Rosewood Knight stood strong, however craven I think him, I am that, methinks, tenfold, and ultimately *he* slew the sorcerer. Single handedly." She laughed. It was shallow, brittle. "*Mayhaps*, when I run from our inevitable altercation, thou can plead with him not to run me down atop with steed and tear me apart with his dogs."

CHAPTER SEVEN

Lorenna Lerelei watched Haera start to gather her things.

"Please don't go," she begged, wringing her hands.

Haera shrugged off her nightgown and Lorenna's grasp, pulling out the pants she had worn the night she had come back. Scars covered her back, blemishing her beautiful brown skin. Their eyes met, and the Selkie turned so that she was facing Lorenna, her back hidden away for only the tower to see. Lorenna grabbed her arm before she could put on a shirt.

"I think they suit you," she said, tracing a finger along one of the jagged, pink cicatrix.

Haera closed her eyes, craning her neck to the ceiling as Lorenna began to kiss each one. "If I can find a cure for you, I'll have to go. These scars… they are a reminder of my own failure. I ran once, but never again." She met Lorenna's gaze. "Make no mistake, my princess, what I do now is not out of cowardice. It is to ensure thy future. Mayhaps my love for you is born of selfish desire. To see myself cure you with my own two hands, rather than the red ones smelling of sickly sweetness."

Haera pulled away, sweeping her hair out after putting on a linen shirt. "I love you!" Cried Lorenna, catching her arm.

The Selkie's hard eyes studied the princess's. "Who is it that your heart longs for more?" She demanded. "The Rose or the Kraken?" Haera shrugged away, pulling on her plates of armor, the shoulder displaying the black tentacles of her house. "Already do I tire of him entering our every sentence. When I return, I hope to cast him from your mind forever. I do not know what you see in him, but I know what I see in you: the power of the sun. Magnificent and beauty so blinding." She sighed, pressing Lorenna's brow against her own. Just for a moment, the subject of the princess's radiance shone through, into her chambers. For that instance, there was nothing but the two women, flesh and heat close together, breaths intermingling, and shadows drowned by glorious sunlight.

"You are the grass softening the land. My brightest star. That which makes the sea warm, when nothing else might."

Lorenna pulled Haera into one last kiss, willing it to last a thousand lifetimes, but knowing one of them would pull away in a matter of moments. "And you are Haera."

The Selkie smiled. Lorenna saw happiness there. A nostalgic feeling. Happiness which could only be achieved by the love of family. There was sadness there, too. A twinge of it, just enough to briefly snuff out the toothy grin she had come to know so well. Once Haera disappeared over the railing, still wearing her flowers that they had picked earlier that morning, and using the thick vines to scale her way down, Lorenna was once again alone.

Over the next hour, the worst feeling she had ever experienced descended upon her. At first, she didn't know what it was. A stabbing inside of her stomach, something desperately clawing, scratching, and biting its way out. It wriggled inside, causing her breakfast to lurch dangerously close to spilling. Her face felt sour, spreading to her lower cheeks and upper neck, threatening to aid the vile creature inside in its attempt to escape. It was loneliness. Terrible, awful loneliness, that which she had not experienced since her earliest memories of her tower. Lorenna realized that all these years, she had been craving companionship, and now it was gone, and the whole world would weep with her.

Also resurfacing in her memory was the little frog that had approached her two days prior, when she had been terribly angry at Mater. Though their interaction had been brief, he had brought Lorenna some small measure of comfort, so much so that she had played along with him, promising knighthood should she ever escape from her spire. Thinking back on it now, perhaps it was cruel to Morrel. Haera was one of the most capable people she had ever known, and Rose even more so, but she was now fighting the urge to hope for the impossible. When the Rosewood Knight first announced that he had located the whereabouts of some cure, she had been ecstatic. So much so that she had failed to consider the daunting task ahead of Haera: a duel with the Rosewood Knight. The man who had slain VVitch single-handedly, and now defied the magyks of the planet by breaking the spell which kept Lorenna in place. Now, Lorenna had to dull her hopes. How could Rose have found such a concoction? Why did it exist at all, if Mater intended for Lorenna to stay in her tower for the rest of her life?

Would I make such a small creature, no more than a child, methinks, my knight? Lorenna mused, casting her dark thoughts away. *My Rose would take offense to that. View it as a mockery of his profession. Though my intentions were pure when I made such a promise, my affirming words were said in vain. Besides, I did not say I* would *make him a knight, only perhaps. It would be unsafe for such a small child to take on that role. In any case, Morrel would be like to forget in a few moons hence.*

Even though she only thought the words, Lorenna's features burned in shame. She could imagine the young marsh frog's look of disappointment, now. An expression of faith lost in a princess whose promises she couldn't keep.

Before she could get too sick, she laid down on her bed, looking at the ceiling. It was plain. A white wood or tile, with cracks running across it. Lorenna imagined it raining down upon her, sharp bits of white splintering her skin, ripping her apart piece by piece until she was a broken husk in an empty tower. Until she was broken, staring up at the black void and pieces of wood and tile filling her mouth, slashing her gums and stabbing her teeth, burying her tongue so she could not speak.

Lorenna was floating. Floating towards a faint light at the end of the darkness. Her feet found solid ground. Cold, and hard, like the memory of a knight fallen in battle. It was still so dark. Her sore teeth chattered, and she fumbled her away around, following the strengthening light. She felt sharp pillars push around her, getting tighter and tighter. Stalagmites squeezed her body until the light was almost gone. They were shifting, the cavern grinding its teeth as Lorenna crawled from out of its belly. Her clothes were ripping. Her fingernails peeling as she pulled her way out of the sharp stone. The light had become pinpricks, and the ocean roared in her ears.

Darkness.

Then,

Sand. Soft and smooth, a warm hand caressing Lorenna's cheek. She blinked. She was lying on a beach, face to the sky. It was orange and red and pink, a beautifully violent swirl of dawn. Craning her neck up, she saw the dark mouth of the cave watching her. Without turning around, Lorenna knew that a vast, black ocean was behind her. Intelligent and glorious, guarding her from the hungry belly of the planet.

Atop the cave, perched on a cliff face with tall, green grass, was a house. Its features shifted, sometimes resembling the curved, arching roofs of the Willowood, sometimes a simple straw hut, sometimes a castle covered in blue roses. No matter how its appearance glimmered in the dim light, Lorenna felt a comforting warmth radiating from it.

She gasped. A hand passed through her. Right through her stomach, like she was nothing more than a memory projected into the wind. Then an arm followed, and the rest of the person walked forward, ignoring her completely. They could not see her. Squinting, Lorenna could not see them. The sun was higher in the sky, now, glaring down upon her eyes. The figure broke into a run, meeting two others at the base of the cliff. They were too distant to see, but Lorenna could see them embrace. A woman's voice rang out, laughing for joy.

Lorenna let out a choked cry of her own. They were family, together again. The memory of them turning and walking up a set of stairs, towards their house, lingered with her as she woke up in her bed, smiling and crying.

Warm, buttery bread had been laid out on a tray next to her, and she dove into it, tearing it apart ravenously. Lorenna no longer was dreaming of splintered teeth and crushing caves. She was at home, eating her favorite food in the world. Drinking deeply from a cup of ice-cold water, she leaned back, sighing. It was still day, so she had not been asleep for very long. Now that she was awake, it was eerie how calmed the tower seemed. She still longed to be outside, more than anything, but Lorenna was uneasy at how comfortable it felt to be safe inside.

The Selkie and the Rose were in a race, now. Both of them speeding to find Lorenna the cure, and both of them no doubt sharpening their blades for their duel. Lorenna liked it not, but the rest of her life hung in the balance of two very determined, strong warriors, minds set on seeing the other fall. Rose was an unstoppable force, and Haera, well… Lorenna hoped Haera would find it within herself to become the immovable object.

"I give you my blessing," Lorenna whispered. For Haera's safety. For Rose's mercy and wisdom. For her freedom.

To the side, Lorenna kept her paints, safely secured inside of wooden buckets, preserved from the outside elements by lids. Prying each of them open, she dragged her bed to the side. It was surprisingly light, despite the queenly size of it. Dipping a brush, coarse from the hairs of plucked statzels, she stood on a stool and began to stroke the tool across the ceiling. Droplets of paint ran down her arms, and occasionally landed on her forehead as she applied it, but Lorenna paid it no heed. From side-to-side, up and down, browns, yellows, and reds washed upon the previously white surface, mesmerizing the princess. Her arms began to burn, and her toes ached from tip-toeing upon the not-quite-tall-enough seat. Still, her eyes never once wandered from the blossoming colors above her.

Then, Lorenna stopped. She lay on the floor, the hard wood beneath her spine, and looked upon her creation. Blinking, she realized she had not known what she was painting until that moment. Her own face rose above her, a corporeal mural of white dress and uplifted chin, white eyes hidden beneath shut eyelids. Behind her hair and antlers, Lorenna's head was surrounded by a lunar eclipse. A cracked, silver circle with a ring of brilliant sun on its outskirts. The fingers on her right hand were closed, save for the index and middle, with the thumb bending, teasing the inside of her palm. Her other hand was kissed by a kneeling Rosewood Knight, adorned in his usual suit of armor. His helm was slightly lifted, so that a handsome pair of lips could brush her hand. On the ground, lower still than Rose, was Haera, grasping at the fringes of Lorenna's dress, as if pining for her attention. There, the three figures stood, watching over the princess.

Lorenna frowned. She would paint it over in the morning.

CHAPTER EIGHT

Morrel the marsh frog beheld the mountain.

It was actually a whole range of them. Spiked rocks, the largest he had ever seen in his entire life, rising out of the ground like scales of a giant serpent, nestled deep underground. It was more than what he had seen in his dream, but he knew it was the right place. The surface shimmered like the Princess Lerelei's tower, but instead of plain, white stone, it was a stone of a million colors. Browns, yellows, reds, and greens, erupting from the ground and bleeding into the purple sky. A flock of tierrans flew above Morrel, their white, feathered tails trailing behind them amongst the pink clouds.

Stroking Deborah's back, he urged the rabbit forward, giddy to reach the place which had cost him the better part of two days to get to. To his shock, Morrel had underestimated the food he would need for the journey, and if his growling tummy could talk, it would agree with him. Bounding across the land, he looked up at the darkening sky. Someone like Mum would say that now would be a good time to rest; build a campfire, toast some mushrooms, maybe put a cup of tea on, if he had a kettle on him, and call it a night.

That was what anyone in the frog grove would've done, but Morrel hadn't left just to bring home on his back. He didn't need to wait until daybreak to climb the mountain. He had Deborah, and his new sword, which had only tried to fly away once. Grabbing the straps of his knapsack, he straightened it, holding his head up high as he faced his final test.

Morrel was still a bit confused on who had visited him in his dream. They looked like Dae, but acted different. They knew more than his friend ever would, as much as Morrel loved him. And the real Dae would not understand his decision. He saw it in his eyes when Morrel had left. Confusion, and worst of all, a little bit of sadness. Then Morrel remembered how he had looked like in his dream. A knight. A true one, not with a wooden armor and sword, but with plates of steel and a sharp blade that glinted heroically in the sunlight.

The trees were strange on the mountainside. They had only two or three branches, splitting off from the main trunk and going almost as tall as the dandelion trees. The branches became thicker than the trunk, leading to bulbs at the very end, blossoming bunches of green leaves. Fog spilled across the rock, and Morrel felt Deborah, whining as she struggled not to slip. This wasn't the rabbit's home. It belonged on the plains of the Heartlands, its paws were not made to climb the hard rock of mountains.

"C'mon, Debbie," he urged, patting the rabbit's fur.

Stomping the ground nervously, Morrel's friend continued forward. The mountain wasn't so steep that he had to keep going on foot. It sloped up, like a great big hill. At least, he hoped it lasted that way all the way to the top. He didn't want to abandon Deborah here, and lose his only friend in the misty dark. He didn't think a rabbit would be able to rock climb.

The trees grew in closer bunches, now. The rock no longer looked as colorful as it had seemed at the bottom. The night had drained away all of its cheerfulness, not even the moonlight painting it blue. Black clouds had covered it, making it seem like Morrel was in a great, dark void, with no up or down, save for where his feet lay planted and his head looked up high, and of course the trees. Tall pillars, moving in the wind, surrounding him on either side. He shivered. Morrel could see his breath.

Then, a tree lay in front of them. Blocking their path. It had not been there before.

Vines clung off of it, swaying and drooping down, nearly touching the ground. It had only one branch, leaning forward and sloping down further than where its main trunk ended. Morrel swallowed, and tried to calm Deborah, who was whining even louder, now. He did not know why, but he felt that something would hear them if he did not quiet the rabbit down. Something that was all too curious as to what was disturbing the nighttime slumber.

"Shhh, Debbie, shh," he whispered, scratching its ear. He tried to keep calm, but his shaky tone of voice must've given him away, because then the rabbit buckled, leaping onto its back legs and throwing Morrel off of its back. "Wait!" He called.

Deborah turned once. Only once, so that Morrel could look the creature in the eye. He could see its eyes wide with fear, but beyond that…

something like the look Daniel would give them when they teased a little too much. Accusatory. *Why did you bring me to this place?*

"I… Daevon said…" Morrel stuttered. He was shivering now. *When did it get so cold?* He wanted to snuggle inside of Deborah's warm fur, but when he looked up again, prepared to meet its eyes, the rabbit was already gone.

Then he saw what had scared it away. What had scared a flesh-eating apex predator away.

The tree had gotten closer. Except… it wasn't a tree at all.

It was a figure, hunched over. A black cloak draped around its gnarled back, a hood obscuring its large head. It resembled the trees quite a bit, but its trunk was a long, crooked torso, legs hidden beneath the black cloth dragging on the ground. Long, greasy hair dripped off of it, matching the vines he had mistook them to be before. Beneath the cowl, white pinpricks that must have been eyes stared at Morrel. Not questioningly, because somehow Morrel knew that it knew more than he would ever learn in his lifetime. Not sympathetically, no. No kind of warmth came from this monster. It was staring at him… hungrily.

"Marshen…" The thing's voice was gravely and low, with a rumble in its throat that sounded as if something was lodged in it. It was deeply accented, but Morrel was still able to understand what it had called him. An ancient name for the frog people. It unfurled a hand from the depths of its garments, its bony arm outstretching a palm, beckoning Morrel with a gray, long-nailed finger.

Morrel drew his sword, trying to keep his hands steady as he held it up, readying himself. He didn't know what this thing wanted with him, but he didn't plan on going down easy. The monster fixed its eyes on the blade, never blinking. "We welcome thee to the house of darkness. Where once great things are now sunken, and we the wretched prithee thine intervention of our godless souls."

"'We'?" Morrel trembled.

He saw them, now. All around him, the trees were moving. The same gnarled, cloaked figures, white eyes digging into his heart. Just below their moans and whispers, he could hear it. Thumping. Thumping. Thumping.

They came closer, all of them reaching out with their gray hands. The one in front of Morrel kept speaking. "Save us, oh brave Marshen! The tearing, black ichor of our Mother Above longs for our return to her Abyssal embrace. Let thee be the savior of us accursed, lichen archetypes. Come, let us feel thine flesh against our palms!"

"Yes!" Another cried. "It has been so long since I have felt the warm touch of another!"

"Please, come closer!"

"Grant we the wretched thine merciful touch!"

"Stay back!" Shouted Morrel. "I'm warning you!" He drew his sword, and the Wretched faltered, backing away a few paces as they eyed his blade. They looked like the white fawns Morrel used to see by the grove, head up and staring at him and his friends when they stepped on a branch nearby. There was always that moment of pause before they ran away, bounding across the red fields. Morrel swung his sword, and the Wretched did not run. They stepped back a little more, but they had formed a perfect ring around him, now. He was trapped.

Where's Dae? Morrel wondered, panicked. *He was supposed to be here. He was supposed to help me become a knight.* He fought down the urge to start crying. He hoped he didn't look like he was about to. Mum could always see his eyebrows stretch, and the lump in his throat holding back tears. It made him angry. These creatures hadn't even done anything, and already he felt like laying down and squeezing his eyes shut, hoping everything would just go away. They were closing in, now. He wasn't some brave knight. He had run away from home. He had run away from his only family in the whole world.

"I SAID STAY BACK!" Morrel roared. His voice echoed across the mountain. The Wretched's tiny eyes widened slightly. The wind whipped around him, pushing at his white cloak. He squeezed the hilt of his sword. It was getting warmer, making his palms so sweaty they threatened to slip right off. With a rush of heat, the metal along the blade burst into flame, first a bright yellow, then an angry red, and finally getting so hot that it was pure white. Morrel didn't wait to see if his hands were getting burned. He felt the angriest he had ever felt in his life. His whole journey – scurrying away in the middle of the night like a rat, facing down the untamed wilds of the Heartlands, making his way up a strange place, so far away from help – all of it would be for nothing if he fell here. These monsters would *not* get in his way.

Without thinking, he charged headfirst into the Wretched right in front of him. The roots from the sword were wrapping around his arm, squeezing it uncomfortably tight, but he didn't care. He stabbed the blade right through the thing's chest, before it could react. With a horrible scream that sounded like forks scraping against a plate, its body seemed to almost melt right then and there. The robes that had been wrapped around it now lay in the dirt, covering a pile of human bones.

One of the Wretched had snuck up behind him. It was holding a long, crooked dagger, ready to strike it directly into Morrel. "Forgive us!" It wailed. "Perhaps our master shall grant thee a death free from servitude!"

Morrel was already swinging his sword back, spinning to face the monster, but he could already feel he was going to be too slow. The dagger was coming down, and Morrel's own blade wouldn't stop his attacker in time.

Then, the roots on his arms shifted. They wriggled like snakes towards his hands, and shot forward, twisting and turning through the air. They formed a tube around the sword, letting the white fire spread onto their trunks. Before the Wretched could react, it was entangled in burning vines. It tried to pry them off of it, but they were too thick, and there were too many. The fire ate the Wretched up, until, just like the last one, there was nothing left but a charred skeleton.

The others tried to put up a fight, too. They all drew rusted daggers or broken swords, but they were no match for Morrel. He could swing his sword, true, but it seemed like the roots had a mind of their own. They writhed and flailed around, scratching and tearing at the beasts until the flames overwhelmed them. Morrel had no idea how his sword was doing all of this, but it felt incredible. He slashed and stabbed as easily as he had wielded a stick back home. Finally, he felt like a true knight of the realm, and finally, all that could see his happy smile were dead around him.

Well, all except for one. The last of the Wretched held him in an unblinking stare. It was laying on the ground, both of its legs cut off at the waist. It wasn't bleeding, but Morrel could see yellow, decomposing bone peeking out from the burned flesh. It smelled like rot and ashes. Morrel pointed his sword at its hidden face. "Yield."

It wheezed, either not able to speak or not wanting to. It dragged itself on the ground, cracked fingernails trying to dig into the earth, peeling away from its fingers when all it met was rock. Morrel looked around. None of the other Wretched were moving. Many of their limbs and other body parts still lay around, surrounded by their robes and bones. His sword was covered in blood, still dripping. Without noticing, the Wretched had cut him in some places. A claw mark scraped it's away across his chest, leaving a bloody tear in his clothes. Morrel's left leg buckled without warning. A nasty gash had opened. It looked like a knife stab.

Hand trembling, Morrel sunk his sword into the Wretched's back before it could reach him. Maybe it was his own, jittery brain making things up, but he could swear he heard the creature rasp "Thank you," before it crumbled away.

The sword was back to normal, now. The white flames no longer covered the metal, and the tree roots that made up the handle didn't writhe and wriggle like lots of big, angry earthworms. Morrel also didn't feel as angry anymore. Scarily angry. He wondered what Mum would say if she saw him like that.

They hadn't even done anything. Not really. All they had done was scare him. Was that enough to make him act that way? Like a tadpole when it didn't get a sweet roll after its supper? Morrel wondered if this was what being a knight was like. Cutting down everyone who stood in your way. After all, he had never stopped to consider the parts of the stories Gramps would tell him, the parts where the dragon died. The dragon never even talked. It never *said* it liked burning and eating people, just like rabbits didn't like eating their prey. It was just something they did, and maybe it wasn't fair to decide that they should die just because they were doing what they had to in order to survive.

He imagined that Daeyvon would say Morrel sounded very much like a grown-up.

There was nothing left to do. Morrel looked around the empty mountaintop. The night was too dark to see very far. He stared south. Dark clouds lined the sky, completely hiding any silver light that might've shone through. He wondered if, on a clear day, he might've been able to see all the way to the grove.

Is this what it feels like to fail? Morrel hadn't always been the best at things, of course. He wasn't the fastest runner among his group of friends, or the highest jumper, or, unsurprisingly, the best swimmer. He knew what it felt like to lose a game to Cadissa or Daeyvon. That was fixed by a round of hide-and-seek, though, which he was also great at, or a great big bowl of soup from Mum. The next day, he bounded right back out the door, ready to have another day of play. Nothing changed, and Morrel forgot about it soon enough. That wasn't failure, though. Now, Morrel understood what the difference was. Failure meant shame. It meant not being able to fix something that you broke. It meant not knowing if he could return home and look Mum in the eye, or telling a princess she could never see the outside world.

Morrel sat down on the ground, leaning on the sword. He buried his head between his arms, not caring that dirt was staining his clothes, or that they were already hopelessly ruined from the battle, already, and it was silly to think about a little dirt. *I came here because of a dream. That was all it took. That was all it took for me to leave my friends, and Mum. What did she say when she found out her only son left her for the wild? What did she think when she found out the last of her family left her all alone?*

Pick yourself up, she had told him once. *Brush off the brambles, and stand back up, Morrel. Do you feel the warm air, from the sunlight beaming through the trees? Do you hear the laughter and song of our people? That doesn't matter to you right now, because of your cuts and scratches. It hurts, and that's all you feel because of it. This isn't always enough for people, but Morrel.* Her voice hardened. *You. Pick yourself. Up. And you don't run away, you face your tears with a smile.*

Flames sparked around him. Not white, like from his sword. Green. From animal skulls chained to poles he hadn't noticed before. They formed a path, twisting and turning away from him, going north. Down the mountainside.

"It *was* a dream, Morrel," said the voice of Daeyvon.

Morrel jumped up. He looked around, but his friend was nowhere in sight. Had he imagined it? How could Dae be all the way out here? He hadn't… followed him, had he? Surely not. Morrel's heartbeat.

"It was a dream, but dreams are magyk." Morrel felt a cold spot on his neck, like a snake coiled around it. He turned around. No one there. "Come visit me. I want to talk face-to-face."

It sounded so much like Dae, just like in his dream back in the grove. Morrel thought that if he got his friend and the voice to both talk at once, he wouldn't be able to tell the difference. That was the point, though, wasn't it? The dream visitor had actually said he wasn't Dae, he just sounded like him so it would be less confusing. Morrel's brows knit together. He wasn't sure that he was any less confused than he would've been if a stranger's voice had spoken to him instead.

Morrel looked at the bodies, and then towards the lighted path. He had to do it. For Lorenna. Maybe his quest wasn't over yet. He squeezed the handle of his sword, hoping it would protect him, and then he walked down to the valley.

CHAPTER NINE

It was half a fortnight later when the Rosewood Knight happened upon the village.

It was a small, runty thing. The ramshackle cottages and dirt lanes reminded him of his dogs. The little ones suckled at their mother's side, so small that Rose once saw the Castellan pick them up by the scruff of their neck and carry them across the yard, as if they were just a small sack of flour to transport. Sometimes they grew into fearsome bloodhounds, other times they fell cold, shivering and nuzzled in their mother's fur.

He blinked, one moment riding deep in the Willowood, past giant trees with red bark obscured by layers of green moss, overshadowed by even larger willow trees, whose leaves dangled like vines, brushing the tops of their redwood counterparts. He turned down a bend in the lane, and he was crossing a wooden bridge, curved and overlooking a trickling stream that churned its way down the hillside. On the other end was the town, cottages with straw roofs and smoking chimneys, the only bricks used for the vine-covered watermill that used the sparse water from the stream to lazily turn its wheel. Though sunlight reflected off the violet sky did manage to peek through the treetops, far above, most of the settlement did not see light, making Rose notice the glowing, blue lichen on the boulders scattered throughout the town, amongst the small, green plants, who's leaves branched from the stem and into the air in spiraling, curled shapes.

Pastures of pumpkins occupied the gaps between houses, as well. Lean, black pumpkins and plump, orange ones, kept by marionettes more unusual than even Windsoar. They were nearly the same size as the cottages, with eight legs planted on the ground, allowing their tube-like mouths to collect the ripe crops. With big, bulbous abdomens, Rose noted that they kept eight more limbs up on top of their bodies, almost perfectly symmetrical to their ground counterparts. Underneath his helm, he scowled. The Rosewood Knight did not wish to be here any longer than he must. Indeed, he planned on moving on, as soon as he found…

There. A marionette that looked humanoid enough. *Not unlike my Castellan, I suppose, though this one is taller and lankier, and undoubtedly more tolerable.* Clearing his throat, he spurred Windsoar over, intercepting the machine before it could venture indoors to some hidden place. "You. Might you have a village lord that I could consult?"

The thing's head whirred as it turned to look at him. Rose did not especially enjoy the empty, black sockets staring up at him. As for clothing, it chose to wear a simple, brown cloak, the hood drawn back, and any trace of its arms obscured beneath its folds. Strangely, the Rosewood Knight found himself hoping that this marionette would not speak to him. He could muster the Castellan's voice well enough, but something about these creatures unnerved him, if one could even call them alive enough to qualify as creatures. They were unnatural. Their appearances did not quite match with the landscape, no matter where across the land he went, and by this point Rose had been to too many a village. He waited breathlessly, and even still did not inhale when the thing lifted a finger from the depths of its clothing, pointing.

Rose followed the marionette's direction, and laid eyes on the lord's keep. If he thought his own keep was lowly, then he had no words to insult this one. It was a house built into the side of a great tree. It contained a sloped, red roof, that almost perfectly camouflaged with the bark of its support. There was no ground beneath it, merely beams of wood that were nailed into the front, then met the tree below, possibly all that kept the house and the ground from colliding with each other. Two oaken doors stood proudly in front, and above them, a huge clock face loomed.

Hardly believing his eyes, Rose asked: "How does one…?"

Again, the marionette pointed, and only then did Rose see the small set of stairs nailed into the side of the tree, spiraling all the way up until they met the doors. He stared up at the keep, considerably higher than all other structures in the small village. The hour was growing late, as was evident by the beams of light slowly draining from the scenery, and the clock hands moving closer and closer to the seven-hour mark. Resigning himself to the long climb ahead, he dismounted Windsoar hastily, not wishing to stay in this place after dark. He was sure that the keep would have good enough quarters, albeit cramped, judging from the size. He was clearly a knight, after all.

Heaving his increasingly heavy armor, he planted one foot in front of the other, leaning against the tree as the only way of banister. To his left was empty air, and the fall was getting harder and harder. This, however, was a tower that he could climb. The steps themselves were logs sawed in half, smoothed, and with a shine applied to them. As he began ascending, his thoughts drifted back to Haera. He should not have bit back at her so obvious bait. He did not wish to turn Lorenna against him, and quarreling with her friend would lead to that conclusion. His blood boiled at the thought of losing Lorenna, but he should have kept his composure. That was what a knight was supposed to do. Still, what was done, was done, and he had a duel to prepare for.

In truth, Lady Haera has more to prepare for than me. One had to have a certain level of skill to be anointed a knight, especially in the Midnight Sea, if the rumors were to be believed. Yet the harsh reality of the Heartlands made for a far greater knightly trial. *And who was the one to slay VVitch, in the end?* That was why Rose allowed himself the time to take on his quest before the duel.

Randomly, Rose turned his head to the bottom of the steps, just in time to see the marionette shift a lever hidden in the tree bark. The Rosewood Knight leaned a hand against the tree as the stairs shifted, moving ever-so-slightly away from the tree, supported by metal beams jutting into a thin space surrounded by the same material that spiraled up the tree, side-by-side with the stairs. They began to move, rising upwards in the same way that Rose would have climbed them regularly. A slight hum emanated from deep within the contraption, and Rose tried not to think about losing his balance as he was guided along by the mechanism. The strong air and wind were attempting to suck him into their embrace, but he didn't plan on letting them.

It was not a lonely summit, however. Here was the domain of things that flew, and they let him know it. Birds sang every which way, filling the air with their high-pitched song. It was not subtle. It was loud, a drawing sound that followed him with every step and sweat. The breeze tugged at his cloak as the song tugged at his sanity.

Nevertheless, the Rosewood Knight made it to the top. By then darkness had taken hold. Firebugs drifted through the air, aiding to the already luminous landscape below. He heard leathery bat wings flap overhead. He used the door knocker, a ring of metal made to look like a crescent moon. *Still, she taunts me.*

The mechanism shifted once more, and the steps slightly retreated into the tree, stopping them from movement. He waited. There was no balcony for him to wait on, only small steps that ended sharply at the door. Rose imagined that because of this, they must open inwards, and yet he stood aside, waiting around the bend of the tree for someone to allow him entrance. He leaned his arms against the rough bark, his back and joints aching. *Pluck the basilisk. Leech the dragon. Gut the warrior. Gut the warrior.* That was the part of the quest that worried him the most. It was not the plucking of the basilisk, which had already been completed. He had been most careful not to rummage in his satchel too hastily. It wasn't even the leeching of the dragon, which was by far the most complicated. The heart of the warrior was what vexed the Rosewood Knight.

Lorenna will surely look distastefully upon me if I mention that key ingredient. She doesn't know how important it is, but it doesn't matter, for she will not like it, and I would not risk incurring the woman's wrath. Not now. Though what luck would it be if my fiercest opponent, Lady Haera, would serve adequately? He chuckled quietly to himself. *Nay, I think not. She is too cowardly. Her heart would not serve. In any case, that is not my most pressing issue at hand, for that is the last step in the de-hexing process. The leeching is what should be my most critical concern.*

Then, finally, the doors creaked open. It was indeed inwards, but only slightly, so that, to his annoyance, Rose was forced to squeeze through the gap. It was like they feared an army waiting for them on the other side, crossbows drawn.

The inside was lit only by a heart on the far end of the room, draping most of the space in shadow. Animal heads were mounted on the wall. None, the Rosewood Knight noted, were of a dragon, though even if marionettes could perform a feat such as dragon slaying, he didn't think they had the appetite to display their trophies. Still, he wondered why these wall mounts occupied the space at all. For the room was bare. An empty floor, save for a bearskin rug near the fireplace, occupied by two simple, wooden chairs, their backs turned to the door. An overlook ran above him, starting from an entrance probably accessed by some tucked away side room, then running along the entire perimeter of the space, both ends stopping as they overlooked the quiet flame. On either side of the hearth, two small doors stood closed. A plain, unlit chandelier hung between beams supporting the tilted roof.

They didn't need to open, for his host was already seated in the left chair by the fire. She wore an enormous, pointed hat, made of brown wrinkled leather, stitched with patches of blue and orange fabric. A shawl covered the rest of her portly body, save for her hands clutching a large volume between yellow fingernails. His relief upon seeing a non-mechanical humanoid quickly subsided, as his eyes met hers. They were hidden beneath folds of soft, spotted flesh, almost as wrinkly as her hat, but they were there. Her body was old, but her mind was not. Dark eyes pierced him, and he felt unnervingly as if she could see beneath his armor and at his nakedness. Involuntarily, Rose shivered.

The crone showed him a toothless smile, cracked lips expanding upwards, but they did not reach her eyes. With shaking, blue-veined hands, she sat the book down, and laid it on her lap. On the cover, Rose read: *Cures for Curses of the Known World.* Her voice sounded as if she was still a maiden, in the accent of a Star Worlder. "Please, sit, Sir Knight. What humble comforts I possess I offer to you now. You may remove your helm, if you so wish. I do not require such formalities in my halls."

Rose sniffed at the word *halls*, but sat down in the chair anyway. He did not remove his helmet, and immediately he knew the woman had taken note of that. She removed a white handkerchief from the depths of her shawl and quietly coughed into it. Though the action was small, Rose could tell that it had taken much out of her. Her temple was beaded with sweat as she dabbed at her mouth and folded it. She adjusted her hat, and he saw short, white hair underneath. She swallowed, the muscles in her neck straining.

"So, you are the knight I have heard tale of. Slayer of the VVitch. My crops have you to thank for it. The black magyk had spread far, to even my village. And now you come in search of a dragon to slay. What curious happenstance that you would wander into my domain."

He shifted in his seat. Though his legs were finally being given a rest, he did not feel comfortable. Eerily, he felt as if it was not happenstance at all. It was impossible, because how could this crone have possibly manipulated events to lead him here, to this backwater village?

As if reading his thoughts, the woman clapped her hands. It was soft, weak, no louder than the far-off death of a star. Yet, soon, Rose heard the clanking feet of a marionette approaching, and to his discomfort, he felt its cold, lifeless hands creep on the edge of the metal plates covering his shoulders. "You called for me, my lord?"

Lord? Rose thought incredulously. *This old one? Truly? At least it's not a marionette running things, though you would think it looking at the state of the place.*

"Yes," the crone purred. "Would you be so kind as to bring some refreshments for our welcome guest? Methinks he is a tea man. Mmm… fetch the kind that we keep stocked in the pantry by the barrels."

"The –?"

"Yes, that one. Mayhaps some biscuits as well. You know how partial I am to the powdered ones."

The marionette bowed. "At once, my lord."

When the thing left, Rose released a breath. He realized he had been holding it. The crone eyed him. "I do apologize for my servants. Though modeled for humans, sometimes they do not contain the subtlety that mannerisms demand. They have more than one use, however, and provide good company, once you look above their quirks."

"Forgive my boldness, my la–my lord. Do you not have subjects other than those of the machine?"

She snorted. "You *are* bold, Rosewood Knight. Yes, I know you did not tell me your name. A move most nobility would sniff at, and one you would undoubtedly curse at yourself for in any other hall, but as I said, I am not one for formalities. Your name is infamous throughout the townships of the countryside, if you are pondering *how* I came across your identity. As for mine, you may call me Lord, or whatever name you have flashing through your mind. I had a name long ago, before your time, I'd wager. Forgotten from memory, now." She leaned forward. "I do wonder why my subjects make you flinch. Could it be that they remind you of the unnatural sorcery of the Witch, I wonder?"

"I presume you have not invited me into your, ah, *home*, to have idle tea and biscuits." Rose had thrown away almost all pretenses of formality, now. The crone was not prone to them, and so he did not owe them to her. Should he not hold back his tongue, she would likely have her minions drag him out and throw him from the tree, but curiosity had the best of him. So, while Rose was not polite, not by any means, he was not brutal, either. Not yet.

The crone leaned back, staring into the flames. "I can aid you in your quest."

"You know where a dragon dwells?"

She slowly shook her head, her hat swaying on top of her skull, as if struggling to stay balanced. "Nay. I can, however, help you summon one."

"Summon one? How would you propose we do that? Pile bodies of flesh in hopes that the beast will smell it come and call? I see no beings to the dragon's taste residing in thy village."

The old woman snickered. "I do not think the marionettes would be to its liking, either. Nay, there are ways. Old ways." From the folds of her shawl, she removed another leatherbound volume. It was green, with hundreds of small patterns carved into it, almost resembling serpent scales. Pages were falling out, sticking out from beneath the cover in various places, wrinkled and yellowed. On the cover, cursive lettering read: *Slaying a Dragon.*

"I've loved reading. Ever since I was a little girl." The crone showed another toothless smile. "Are you a literary man, good Sir?" The lettering for *Cures for Curses* glinted in the firelight.

She's taunting me. This VVitch is making a jape of me. Rose dismissed the thought as soon as it passed through his head. *Nay. She is worming her mannerisms into my mind, making me believe she uses sorcery to foul the planet.* "I unfortunately find myself lacking time for such ventures most days."

This time, the Rosewood Knight saw the door creak open, and the crone's servant creeped in once again. In its hands, it carried a tray, containing an ornate teapot, with a white base color engraved with flowery, silver designs. Two cups were stacked on top of each other, and next to them, biscuits had white sugar powdered on top. In the marionette's other hand, it carried a small table, which it sat down in front of the fire where it laid the refreshments.

The crone poured herself a cup and stirred it with a spoon, the metal slightly clinking against the sides. Rose did not move. "How do you plan on luring this great beast?"

She blew at the steam rising from the hot tea. "Though these creatures themselves are creatures of fire, dragons always crave more.

Whether it is to physically consume it, or stare hypnotically into its depth, is unknown. In any case, we have no shortage of wood in this village, and you may just be the flint to strike the spark."

Now Rose reached for the tea. He was growing tired, and did indeed crave the warm drink. Stirring sugar into the liquid, he looked at the ancient sack of skin and bones sitting across from him. She was not to be trusted. Not at all. However, if she might help him further his own needs…

"Why are you helping me? I am but a simple knight, come to your home, and you are so ready to aid him? You said that this dragon is not an immediate threat to your realm, so what need have you of a dragon slayer?"

He saw the crone's eyes flicker back to the fire, and he raised his helm, so that he might drink. The aroma was slightly sweet, like the springtime when the land was in bloom. When the tea met his mouth, the Rosewood Knight nearly spat it out. It had an acidic, bitter taste. The sweet smell did not reflect the flavor at all, what little flavor there even was.

He fixed his helm as the crone regarded him again. "I am but a simple servant of the Moon's Blood and her Sun-Bright Child." She looked at his cup. "Rose tea. Is it to your liking?"

CHAPTER TEN

Morrel the marsh frog felt the gathering darkness.

The green lights behind him were being snuffed out, one by one. Whether it was the wind, or some sort of magyk, Morrel didn't know, but he tried not to shiver as another pair of the strange lanterns went out with barely a snuff. The path was slowly leading him down the mountain, twisting and turning as it thankfully avoided the steeper cliff edges. Invisible to the eye even in daylight, only shown to him now through the illumination of the green lights. Morrel didn't want to think about what would've happened if he tried to get down here on his own, without the flames shining the way forward. Not that he likely would've gone down here at all, if not for the flames showing up when they did. Still, it was too late. He had to do this. For the princess.

The trees began to turn into old, rotting oaks. The pretty, rainbow stone of the mountainside turned to hard gravel and dirt. He wished right now that Deborah was here with him. It would be nice to have a friend in the dark forest. Instead, he was alone, with only the shadows to keep him company, and the voice that called itself Daeyvon. Those, and the shapes rising from the water.

The water was murky. A black, oozy film covered it, probably a home for all sorts of insects and creepy-crawlies. As his feet touched the bottom, the sand and mud below felt almost wobbly, like it was just another layer on top of an even deeper black, void. None of that really mattered to Morrel at the moment. He drew his sword, arms burning from lifting and using it all day. It didn't wrap around his arm, this time. Even though it had been scary, it had also been… powerful. Useful. For once, a little frog could be just as strong as the giants around him.

Two huge serpents looked at him. Seaweed and muck hung on to their slimy bodies, making it look like they had tangled, dirty beards. A rattle lay on the ends of their tales, filling the air with a warning for Morrel not to get any closer. Their sharp, white teeth glinted in the night. Forked tongues flicked in and out, tasting the air for their next meal. Between them, the water bubbled. Morrel braced himself, waiting for their third brother to lash out from the swamp, saying hello with its gaping mouth.

It never came. Instead, a round, round-eared head rose out of the water. It was completely covered in black mud, so Morrel couldn't make out who or what it was. At least, not at first. The figure kept rising, dark ooze sticking to them from head-to-toe. When they opened their eyes, they were wide, thoughtful.

"B-be you man, or selkie?"

He smiled a mouth of white teeth. "Neither." The serpents smothered him, slithering around the newcomer's body so that the mud was washed off, leaving...

"Daeyvon?" Morrel asked, his voice barely above a whisper.

The serpents backed off, standing on either side of Morrel's friend like two bodyguards. Daeyvon stroked one of their necks, body naked and exposed to the elements, though he didn't seem to care. "Not Daeyvon, remember?"

"But..." Morrel squeezed his sword tighter, looking nervously at the snakes.

Not Dae looked at them, as if just remembering that they were there. "Oh, these? They won't... kill anyone unless I tell them to. Thou have naught to fear, little Marshen."

Morrel shivered. That was what the Wretched had called him, too. "Why do you look like him? Sound like him? I know you said it was to make things less confusing, but... is this sorcery?"

"Souls have called it by that name, yes." He studied Morrel with a stare that was so intense he had the urge to look away. "Are you still on thy illustrious odyssey?" For a moment, his voice changed slightly, from the low-born, braggy tone that Morrel had heard Dae use so often, to a deeper, accented one.

"Do you have the Princess Lorenna's cure?"

"My boy, I have the *means*." It was very strange for someone who looked about Morrel's age to call him a boy. Like he was just a little child. One who wandered too far from home. "The mountain was a test. I heard your mighty ambition. Your *desire*. I knew you were the perfect warrior to carry out the quest, and your bravery up on the mountain confirmed it."

Morrel looked down at his sword again. "I thought they were going to hurt me."

Not Dae nodded. "And you stopped them." He also looked at the weapon. "That instrument – what did it tell you?"

Morrel looked up in surprise. "It can talk?"

Not Dae chuckled. "Not in the way you and I are, perhaps. It showed you what you are capable of. Your unbridled potential. As a knight. As Lerelei's greatest warrior."

"Really?" The sword was normal. Just a blade buried deep in a handle made of tree roots. A weapon Morrel had found sleeping in the earth. Then again, the Selkie's sword looked normal, too, and she was chosen by the princess to be her knight. He imagined himself again as a knight. Tall, in shining armor.

Morrel straightened himself. "I'm doing this for Princess Lorenna. A true knight is selfless."

Not Dae sneered. "Mayhaps the Codex should have been written by you."

"I don't need a Codex to know that. Tell me how to cure the princess. I'll make sure no one else has to get hurt."

The snakes hissed. Not Dae's next words felt as cold as the water around Morrel's ankles. "Your heart, Morrel. The beating innocence of a noble warrior. Magyk is not without its cost. It needs… life to practice, and so ambitious a spell will cost you yours. Tell me, what would a knight do? Sacrifice their own life? Even if it meant they never saw their loved ones again? Even if it meant their loved ones never saw *you* again? Marshen, what would thyself do in the name of honor?"

Morrel felt dizzy. He looked down at his chest, still bleeding from the fight with the Wretched. *Had they known? Had they been trying to get my heart? Use it to free themselves from whatever still kept them tied to the planet?* Even worse, he had come all this way, made the Princess Lorenna endure even more time in her prison, while the cure had been within his reach all along. Within *him* all along.

What was he to do? He had a responsibility to the princess, first and foremost, right? He had to free her. He had to. *But are you really doing it for her, or because you want to become a knight?* A little voice in his head nagged.

Could Morrel really do that to Mum? Make it so she never saw her son again? Lose the only family she still had left?

He felt the sword stir. The roots started creeping around his arm. He would find another way. *He would.* Grandad would not want him throwing away his life like that. Morrel would live to fight on for… was it honor, as the thing that looked like Daeyvon had put it? Or was it something else? Something deeper? "Sorry," Morrel said, addressing Not Dae. He had begun to look a little pale. The skin on his brow twitched, like he had a bad headache. His ears were peeled back, like a rabbit. "I think I'll find another way."

The snakes started moving forward, but Not Dae held them back. His smile looked twisted, like he was trying hard not to scowl. *Has he gotten taller?* "*You* are the key, Marshen. Without you, Lorenna Lerelei has no hope of escaping her spire."

Morrel breathed deeply. "I need to see my mum first. I need to see Daeyvon. I need to tell them I'm alright. I won't run away again. If it really only ends with me, then I'll get their blessing first."

In three quick steps, and before Morrel could do anything, Not Dae was leaning over him. His breath smelled. His nostrils were flared. His skin was no longer green, but very pale, like some humans. "You don't need to die, Morrel. As a knight swears an oath to their lord, pledge yourself to me. Even without a heart, you will still walk on this planet. Only if you pledge, I can do this. What you call magyk is limited within me, and only adheres to certain rules. You need not abandon everything, Marshen, just your loyalty to your princess."

Morrel let himself think about it for one moment, and then no more.

"Like your Wretched? Walk the earth like that? That's not living. That's another tower to never come down from." He pointed his sword at the VVitch. "Now let me go in peace. I don't want to hurt you."

VVitch laughed. It was tainted, garbled. Fully affected by the foreign accent that had slipped out before. He was a bald, slimy man. No longer what looked like Daeyvon the marsh frog. "The child threatens the one who taunts Abyss."

The two snakes dashed forward, at speeds that would've overtaken Morrel had they actually been aiming for him. Instead, they stopped at

VVitch's side, long enough for him to grab their necks with two meaty hands. Crushing them, he bit his mossy teeth into their skin, blood running down his chin. Morrel backed up as he grew. And grew. And grew. "Calkrula gon Eekid," he chanted, in an old language. "I have need of a warrior such as thou, little frog. Thy shall be the finest of my Wretched! Untainted by weakness! Untainted by personal ambition! By rot!"

Morrel did run. He ran faster than he ever had in his whole life. The green flames around him blazed white, and he could feel his sword growing, swallowing his arm. The trees groaned with a strengthening breeze. Cold air whipped at his ripped clothing, but Morrel barely felt it. He only felt the need to get out. *Do knights ever get scared?*

"The others – like so many of this planet – fear me. Fear my power. They keep me from my home world. Banish me and my creations. My weapons and my forsaken lich. Let me use what they so feared, now. I call upon the power of dead gods –!" His words were caught by a scream. It hurt so much Morrel pressed his ears with his one free hand, tripping and rolling on the ground. He had made it to the edge of the mountainside. Hard rock pressed against his back, and water licked his feet.

When he opened his eyes, he didn't understand what he was seeing at first. It was the Vvitch – huge, half as big as the mountain itself, with glowing, white eyes, and a watering mouth of sharp teeth. Except where his legs had once been, were long, hairy, black stalks. Two sets of four, each on either side of him, scraping and crawling on the ground as they tore their way through the forest. Behind him, a bulbous abdomen with an ugly looking stinger on the end swayed back and forth. Birds flew from their nests, escaping the giant monster that now stomped through their home, and bigger things, too. Things that hummed in worry. Rocks rolled down the mountainside, shaken loose by the stomps of the VVitch's feet. By some miracle, none of them hit Morrel, but that was definitely the least of his worries as he stared down the ancient nightmare, unable to make himself move now that he had fallen.

VVitch's eyes rested on the sword in Morrel's hand, wrapping vines around him like a suit of armor. "And mine own creations turn against me, gifts turned into foreign property. The poisoned apple turned to delicacy." He reared up, preparing to stab down with a pincer-like spider leg. "No more deals. No more idle plotting. The planet shall see me for which I am: their new king, and you, Marshen, will be my general."

The sword's roots wrapped around the leg just as it came crashing down. Even though it wasn't exactly attached to him, Morrel still felt the weight of the VVitch, threatening to crush him. He watched as the claw came closer and closer, pressing down despite the tangle of vines that stopped it from immediately killing him. Morrel reached with his other hand, letting the roots take hold and use it to support the column that held the VVitch back. Before his feet could slip on the rocks, the roots swirled around his legs, widening at the ankles to make tree stems that stuck him to the earth.

One,

two,

three.

And Morrel hunched over, pushing his spine against the tree roots covering his back. Instead of resisting, they moved with him. He moved one arm free, then the other. His white sheet had been completely torn, now, the majority of it tied to his neck, flapping in the wind, and the only other thing covering him was the oaken armor. The roots held strong, still, even as the VVitch used more of his body to press down. Roots still twirled around him, small ones attaching him to the mass that shouldered the VVitch. In one thought, they moved aside for his feet to step out of.

Morrel looked at the mountain. They could keep the VVitch in place long enough for him to escape. He could warn people about the giant that was about to peek its head above the mountains. Maybe save some of them before it was too late.

Then, he looked up at the VVitch, and he began to climb. Not like he would climb a rock, exactly. He kept his feet planted on the roots beneath, and leaned upright, letting the vines hold him up and stop him from falling down. Holding the sword in one hand, he focused on walking up to the VVitch's torso, testing each footstep, and finding that they never failed him. After a few more casual steps, he began to speed up, getting used to suddenly walking vertically upwards. Then, Morrel was running. Running towards VVitch's terrible face, concentrated on putting an end to the frog that had made it all this way.

Once he noticed Morrel running up his leg, he swung an arm at him, and Morrel ducked, just barely avoiding the claw-like nails swiping the spot where his head had once been. He shook the leg covered in squirming tree roots. Morrel squeezed two loops that formed in front of him, acting like handlebars. They curled around him, making sure he stayed on even as his legs flopped around as VVitch shook and shook. When the monster paused to take a deep breath, a rattling sound that blew wind all around him, Morrel kept running up. As he ran, he scraped his sword against VVitch's skin, hoping to keep him distracted for long enough so that he wouldn't keep squishing the land underneath them, and so Morrel could reach his head.

Each time the VVitch moved, more and more roots broke off, unable to find a good foothold since it was smooth skin they were growing on, and not the dirt and rock filled with crevices and holes. Underneath Morrel, there were little roots between him and the long drop to the ground.

He reached the cold, clammy skin of the torso. He slowed, using the sword as a pick, stabbing into the VVitch's belly so that he could use the handle as a thing to grab onto as he climbed. VVitch roared in pain, bringing another hand down on Morrel. He closed his eyes, pressing himself against the skin. It was moving too fast for him to avoid, and this time VVitch was scratching himself, allowing no space between him and his body, so that no matter what Morrel would be caught and flung into the air, or squeezed in the VVitch's cold grip.

Instead of getting turned into a pancake, Morrel heard VVitch howl in pain again. He stumbled slightly, rocking Morrel back and forth. He was trying to shake someone off him on the ground below! They were clinging onto one of his claws, refusing to get off no matter how hard he shook. Morrel stared in amazement. Who could it be? Had someone really followed him this deep into the mountains? Someone willing to risk everything?

Then, he saw them for who they were. They were too big to be a human, frog, or marionette. Their bite was strong enough to cause a creature of VVitch's size real pain. Deborah the rabbit furiously chewed away at VVitch's foot, hanging on from just the strength of its jaw. Morrel swallowed. He was glad he had never been on the rabbit's bad side. They locked eyes, and even though Deborah couldn't speak, Morrel understood it anyway.

While VVitch was focused on the rabbit, the roots had creeped forward, covering half of his torso in twisting wood. With one final push off with his feet, Morrel charged, pointing his sword forward. His own yell was covered by VVitch's thunder, but it didn't matter. He just needed one final step. One more. Just… one… more.

And then, Morrel stood on the VVitch's head. He looked down on the world around them. Dawn was breaking, peeking over the mountains, but he didn't see the splash of color that surrounded the VVitch's valley. He saw the shattered forest. The crumbling mountainside. Deborah lying limp on the ground by the VVitch's foot, and the foot rising, its shadow covering Morrel's friend.

Morrel did not need to look into the VVitch's eyes before he plunged his sword down. White flames shot across the vines covering his ginormous body, arching in zig-zags, spirals, and swirls. They arched across a vine curled around Morrel's arm, infusing the blade of the sword in smoke and fire. Blood blossomed from his head, dripping into his eyes. He wailed and wailed as his body burned, forgetting about the rabbit at his feet. Morrel turned away as his sword got brighter and brighter, making the night sky turn whiter than clouds.

Then, he felt its handle leave his hands. He felt his feet leave the scalp-y surface. Felt the wind rushing around him. When Morrel opened his eyes, he saw the VVitch, burned spider body and all, hanging limp in the air. Above him, a shadow blocked out the moon. A circle that kept on going and going, reaching the edges of the horizon, and at its center, the same white light that had come from his sword beamed down on the VVitch, pulling him upwards in a rod of luminescence.

Luminescence. Morrel had never used that word before.

He saw the glint of his sword disappear into the clouds, then heard the VVitch's panicked, crackling voice. "I am not dead! So long as you, or mine own kin, allow me to live, I will cause misery upon this world! Ettiah herself is powerless to stop me. Not all of the armies of man could!" He began laughing, and laughing, until he was swallowed by the circle.

The light dimmed, and Morrel watched the circle start to spin, slowly at first, then faster and faster, creating a hypnotic image in the sky:

stars seemingly swirling around a black void. Then, it was gone, and the moon was the only thing that remained.

It was daytime. Deborah nuzzled Morrel, making him come back to the present. The rabbit was covered in bruises and blood darkened its fur, but it was still standing. They both were. Even the forest around them didn't seem so dark now.

"Come on," Morrel said, patting Deborah's back. "Let's go home."

CHAPTER ELEVEN

The Rosewood Knight tried his best to go to sleep.

By all rights, he should be exhausted. The long ride to the village had taxed him, and the climb up the stairs combined with the conversation with the old woman even more so. Perhaps it was the mattress under his back that may as well have been a slab of stone, in a small chamber unnoticed at the back of the keep. Or perhaps it was that Rose was so close to completing his quest. Soon he would have the dragon's blood, and he would be one step closer to ridding Lorenna of her elevated chains.

Rose pressed a cold cloth against his head, closing his eyes for the hundredth time since he had laid down. It did nothing to quell the pounding behind his eyes, and his endless deliberation with the marionettes on whether he wanted a cold or a hot rag hadn't helped, either. Growling, he sat up, using a free hand to take a swig from his canteen. Even though he had the drapes closed around his window, it didn't do much to silence the forest around him. If he assumed that the night would quiet the local wildlife, he was sorely mistaken. Though the Heartlands was mostly barren, it at least offered peace when he needed it.

He lit a candle on the bedside table. Red wax dripped off of the wick, trying to run away from the bright flame. It pooled at the base of the black candle holder, making a puddle of hot goop. It cast the room in dim light, and he turned away from looking directly at it, still nursing his brow.

Can the crone be trusted? Will she truly aid me in slaying this dragon? Rose didn't like the looks of her. Something about the way she regarded him made him on edge, and there was that tea… He supposed he would find out soon enough if it had been poisoned or not. It had been foolish of the Rosewood Knight to readily accept beverage from her. He relied on his instincts too much, and sometimes they made him do unwise things. Yet, they always pulled through for him, too. It hadn't entirely been wisdom that had felled the basilisk. Rose had felt the need to lure it out into the open, and so he followed that need. Was following want such a bad thing?

Someone knocked at the door. Rose scowled. "Who comes to my chamber entry at this hour?"

"Apologies, good Sir," came the reply of one of the crone's mechanical servants. "The light underneath thy door was made aware to me. I came to offer my services, should they be needed."

The Rosewood Knight stood, leaning against the closed door. "First you burn my tea," he grumbled, "then you disturb my rest. No, I have no need of thy self."

The marionette paused. "Forgive me, Sir, but it 'twas not burned. I am certain of it. Perhaps you were just unaccustomed to the taste –"

"How would you know what anything tastes like?" Rose knew he should not engage with the marionette, but they had a way of getting under his skin, and he was not pleased to be indoctrinated into hyperbolic tea time with this machine.

"I would not."

"There, you see? I do not know how your lady runs her village, but in my keep my castellan shows respect."

"Forgive me –"

"Bah! Forgiveness is all my castellan asks for, as well. I am not some warmonger who demands worship. Why do you treat me so?"

"Perhaps it is the ballad of thy mannerisms, not thy speak."

Rose's eyes narrowed. "What would you know of my mannerisms? The doings you imply ill of are the very ones which will rid your region of dragon. That has slain VVitch and brought an end to plight and chaos."

"You are right, Sir. I know of few things. Only that of gears and masks."

"Begone. I have no need of thy self."

He heard the marionette walking away, hard feet clattering against the wood floor. Rose slid down to the floor, resting his arms on his knees. He looked to his sword and armor, resting next to his bed, ready to be donned should the need present itself. Rose's limbs felt heavy from the days of hard riding across the countryside. This night was the first he had slept in a real bed, and not the ground of his makeshift campsites or the straw beds of the rare inn. Even then, he tended to avoid those kinds of places, since the marionettes demanded much coin, on account of the lack of visitors. Rose wondered why they bothered with coin at all. It wasn't like they needed to eat, and from what he had seen they took no joy in the comforts that came with riches.

He swatted away a fly that was buzzing next to his ear. He imagined that the Lady Lorenna was staring at the stars, now. Leaning against her balcony as she always did, caressing her hands against the pristine, white surface. Rubbing her fingers across the cracks and crevices, slipping them around the pillars that ran around the railing. Laying on the floor when it was sunny out, spreading her legs across the cool surface, and closing her colorless eyes. Rose's mind drifted to the black vines reaching for Lorenna, coiling around her wrists and ankles, keeping her in place. She opened her eyes, startled, and tried to let out a noise, but a thicker vine wrapped around her mouth, gagging any attempt at speech. The vines squeezed her, pressing her head to the floor so she couldn't lift it. The thorns cut into her palms, spilling blood. It pooled, staining the tiles and her gown.

The Rosewood Knight opened his eyes. He could still hear her muffled gasping. Feel the wetness of the blood on the floor. He crawled back into bed, blearily wishing he could continue the dream, if so just to be able to sleep. Despite himself, Rose thought back to Brimeor. His fallen compatriot. They had met not too far away from the valley of the VVitch. Fighting ferociously against the VVitch's minions, the two knights had just barely made it out of the mountains with their lives. Lorenna had not needed to convince him much to go back with Brimeor and Haera for a rematch with the wærlock. In the end, Rose had come out victorious, had he not? Without Brimeor. It did him no justice to dwell on something that could not have been changed.

It did do him justice to look to the future. His duel with Haera was coming, and Rose did not expect it to end peacefully. He had brushed up on his sword fighting, but had she? Had she grown any more courageous since their fight with VVitch. If not, then she was foolish to challenge him to a duel. If she had, then she was foolish *and* confident.

Dawn was coming soon. Rose turned to his side, trying his best to catch some sort of sleep before the day arrived, bringing forth dragons and headaches. He could still hear the fly, buzzing somewhere close by to him. When he opened his eyes, all he saw was the night sky, strangely devoid of stars.

CHAPTER TWELVE

The crone delivered on her promise, much to the Rosewood Knight's uneasiness.

The pyre was constructed of dozens of wooden logs, piled into a pyramid. Surrounding them were the lichen-covered boulders, keeping them in place. Without them, they would probably slide off, crushing all beneath them.

They stood at the tip of the hill, a good way's up from the village, which was terraced on its side. The top had been flattening and cleared, making the trees end abruptly and the open sky begin. The ground was mostly dirt, with clumps of red grass growing in odd patches.

Unnoticed by Rose in the dark the previous night, the back of the keep had a tunnel that ran straight through the tree, leading to an elevator constructed from pulleys and a flat, wooden platform. From there, the crone was lowered to the ground, as the steps would definitely have proven too much for her knees. Through the day, a procession of marionettes slowly carried the old woman atop a palanquin. It was part of the lift from the keep, removed from the ropes that held it aloft. A huge, purple cushion was placed on it. Rose had accompanied the procession atop Windsoar, escorting them from the flank. When they finally reached the hilltop, the sun was at its peak.

Now, the old woman sat on the ground, her palanquin resting against the earth. She wore a black, puff-sleeved dress, with a matching sun bonnet. A veil covered her face, though he could still make out her piercing eyes through the thin fabric. Rose and the servants stacked the wood on the pyre. Flies and other insects clung onto the pieces of lumber as they removed them from their stacked position at the edge of the clearing, beneath a stone shelter, to protect it from the rains. Briefly, the Rosewood Knight wondered how flammable the marionettes were. They looked wooden enough.

As they constructed the enormous bonfire, only stopping for Rose to take swigs out of his canteen, and for the crone to insist on luncheon, the stack grew. When they were finished, the sun was already lowering between the trees. The day had passed building the dragon trap. Rose stepped back, surveying his work, and nodded. He did not know exactly how this would lure the dragon, but the deed was done. It was nine meters in height, and towered over all in the clearing.

Unnoticed, the crone had slowly walked over to Rose, as she now stood behind him when she spoke. "Does she know about your quest?"

He should not have been surprised that this old woman knew about Lorenna. "She does."

"How noble. And asking so… little in return."

Rose bristled. "When do we light the pyre?"

The crone looked at the sky. Her eyes squinted through her folds of veiny skin, looking past her veil. "When Ettiah's Sun-Bright Child has set. Ahmer is who we pray to now, Rosewood Knight. They are the dictator of fire. The king of dragons. At least until the Moon's Blood lays dormant in the sky, though she is late tonight."

"Your gods mean nothing to me. I need the blood of this dragon, so pray as you must, just bring me the means." He looked down at her cooly. Rose dwarfed the old woman in size.

She pursed her lips together. "Does confidence come from the body, or the blade, I wonder? Ah, you scoff now, but when you reach my age you find other weapons to demolish your enemies."

"What enemies? Your servants? The woodland squirrels? Best leave the dragon to me. I do not think books will be sufficient to slay the beast."

The crone tilted her head. "As you say." Once again, she looked up at the sky. "Methinks the time has come." She let out a sharp whistle. Immediately a marionette marched over, wearing a tattered, red cloak, swooped so that it covered one shoulder. "Cerre, would you do the honors?"

Wordlessly, the mechanism nodded, and marched over to the hovel where the wood had previously been kept. It produced a torch, unlit. Rose stepped forward. "Let me do it."

The crone waved for the mannequin to hand him the tool, and it obliged. Rose reached into his satchel, briefly fingering the feather, before producing a flint. Finding himself before the pyre, he knelt to its base, and began to strike. Four times he struck it, and produced nothing but a hint of smoke. Four times, muscles burning. Four times, Rose keenly aware of the mannequins standing motionless on the edges of his vision, in a large circle around the pyre. The fifth time, when he struck the flint, fire was born.

Immediately he shoved his hand into the depths of the wooden pyramid so that the flame could be nourished, and stood so as to watch his work come to life before his very eyes. Rose was almost in awe as the structure almost as tall as his keep began to erupt into red and orange and yellow. Above the crackling, Rose heard the singing before he heard the running.

The singing was ugly. A woman's voice echoing through the air like a fog horn beckoning ships to jagged, cold rocks. It warbled in tone, but only grew louder and louder behind him, until he realized that it was the crone herself trilling. Then, Rose heard the running footsteps. Crushing the sand and pebbles in the soil beneath light feat. It was clattering, almost like it was made of wood.

The Rosewood Knight knew it was too late to turn around. Instead, he reached his arm to where he had his shield mounted on his back, and unclasped it. With a surge of adrenaline, he crouched, then slammed the shield upwards as the mannequin descended upon him. He heard the body hit the ground, and turned. There it was. The wooden puppet, the one called Cerre, cowering on the ground, incapable of speech and producing a strange moaning sound, only just noticeable above the hag's intolerable screeching. His shield was pointed at the bottom, and so he brought it crashing down like a blade, splicing the marionette's arm and pinning it to the ground, unable to crawl away in one last desperate bargain with what it called life. Rose grabbed its other shaking arm and tore its body away, leaving the other arm beneath the shield, which he himself left embedded in the ground. He dragged the construct over, and uttered: "Feed the fire," before shoving the marionette in.

The flames grew hotter and brighter. He turned back to the hag, who was still singing, her arms raised to the air, as if clasping at the stars. By now, it had grown completely dark. It was just him, the shadows on either side, the fire behind him, and his sword raised, descending upon this lord of dolls. Then, *Last One* struck metal, and Rose did not understand.

"VVitch!" He spat. "Trying to end me was your first and last mistake. You should have kept your crooked nose in your books." Rose pressed down harder, but the blade would not budge. She was still singing, gazing up to the heavens. *Your foul sorcery will break,* he promised silently. Then, his eyes realized.

It was not an invisible force that addled his sword. It was another blade, and one he had seen before. The longsword of Haera, Knight of the Midnight Sea.

"It is as it was written!" The crone babbled. "The one who follows! The contender to Lerelei's hand!"

With almost incredible ease, she deflected the point of his broadsword towards the ground. She wore her brilliant-green armor, her helm lowered and gazing directly at his own. In her other hand, she held her oval shield. Before Rose had a chance to think, she was advancing.

He backed away, flicking his sword in his wrist to keep it nimble. He wrenched his shield from the ground and held it ready. *Words first, action last.* "What are you doing? She was trying to kill me! A trick to feed us all to the dragon, no doubt."

She made no answer. Instead, Haera swung the blade at his own, clanging off the steel with a painful reverb. He realized that she was backing him towards the fire, and turned so that his left side was facing the flames and she her right. They gazed at each other. This time, Haera didn't make a move.

Rose laughed. "Still craven, I see. Mayhaps you can join the old one in her reading, should I spare your life." He clanged his sword against his shield. "Is the warrior of the Roaring Dark too craven to finish her fight?" The glowing circles etched into *Last One* were invisible compared to the firelight.

He heard a loud creaking, and before he knew it, a large thing had descended upon the Rosewood Knight. He threw himself to the side just in time to avoid the tree crushing him flat. It landed in the fire, creating an explosion of sparks, and thick, black smoke as the flames began to lick its bark. The brief swell of the pyre allowed him to catch a glimpse of the marionettes backing away into the forest, two of them clutching the saw blade which had felled the tree. How they had accomplished cutting through the monolith was beyond him. Turning around, he saw Haera staring at him from the other side of the tree, before the smoke covered her. He could feel the heat. It was coming for him. Worming itself in between his armor and suffocating him.

Rose lifted his sword just in time to block a descending Haera, leaping from the grayness, wreathed in smoke and ember, even momentarily forming shapes behind her shoulders that resembled a pair of jagged wings, just as an Eclipser of ancient times. The impact of metal drew its own sparks, and for a moment the two knights were nothing more but constructs of silver steel and red flame. Rose slid his blade to aim for her legs, but she met it yet again, forcing it into an arch that landed with it kissing the ground. He used the new position to dig the point of his sword into the soft dirt, kicking it up towards her face. She stumbled back, spitting and closing her eyes. He barreled into her, aiming to use his hard armor to shove against the flames now completely enveloping the tree. He hated being so close to the fire, but he had no choice.

"Through smoke and flame, the gaze eternal of Moon's Blood shall be rendered blind!" The crone preached.

Haera hit him in the back with the pommel of her sword, and Rose grunted, losing his momentum. She wriggled free and slipped away yet again into the smoke, seemingly un-choked by its voluminous tendrils. Rose heard her yell above the inferno: "I know when I am outmatched. I was waiting for *that.*"

Two things happened, just then: Rose realized he could see Haera by the roots of the tree, cloaking herself in shadow; And he saw her pointing. For a split second, he thought she was lying, attempting to pettily distract him so that she could get a good swing in. All he saw was the glowing embers rising into the night sky, contrasting the brilliant, silver moon, rivers of black running across its surface. That was all there was, and the small dot on the horizon, illuminated only by the celestial body. Rose realized too slow for what it was.

The dragon was emitting a strange, humming noise. A buzzing so loud he thought that all of Willowood could hear. The creature was getting closer, and he could make out the flutter of fast wings. Rose saw Haera's sword coming for another strike, and yelled as his instincts kicked in, blocking the strike with his arm. It was armored, yet the bite of the blade slid off the steel and sliced his flesh in the kinks of the metal plating.

"Don't you want to save Lorenna?" Rose grunted between strikes, as he blocked and parried. "I need the dragon's blood to cure her. Don't you wish for her to feel the grass? *See* the land that she rules? Truly see it?"

They were slowly making their way around the perimeter of the pyre, hacking and slashing at each other. The Rosewood Knight brought his shield crashing down on her boot. Haera screamed. As she fell to one knee, she slammed the handle of her sword into his chest. He staggered back.

She stood up. "*Her* lands?! Truly?! I can climb her tower, Rosewood Knight. She is trapped, yes, but we are content. How would you have it? You her king as you lock Lorenna away in your miserable little keep? If she were to love you not would you make her drunk on love pots? Maybe I will wait for the dragon to kill you right here, then leech the thing as it is feasting on your corpse."

The crone began to say something else, and Rose broke away. He dashed towards her, grinding his teeth. *She'll pay. She would dare assassinate me? That hag's pathetic life will end at the tip of my sword. This VVitch shall pay, oh, I swear it.*

The old hag looked at the sky, her words drowned by groaning wood in the fire. Two more marionettes dashed from out of the trees. One wore a gray rag over its left eye, the right side of its face covered by a smiling white mask. It brandished a black war cleaver. The second machine wore a green, leather vest, made for the outdoors. Its pants had been fashioned from the white fur of a dire bear, and it held two crooked daggers. Covering its head was a hood, made of the same furs. They dangled down to its shoulders, creating a preposterous imitation of a person. These marionettes certainly had not been with the main party when Rose had accompanied them up the hill. Further proof that the crone had planned this from the start, hiding murderers in the trees to finish him off.

The one with the cleaver reached him first. It swung the weapon at his side, whistling through the air. He easily side-stepped it, readying his sword once more. The marionette looked at him. "I am Uhuria. Know my name well, Rosewood Knight, for it will be the last one that you will ever hear."

Another one with a name. He raised his weapon, and pain arched through his arm as the marionette with the daggers slashed at the open space in between the metal plates. Rose elbowed it in the face, cracking its mask. As his arms were drawn back, he caught the blade of the cleaver just before it struck his helm. The marionette still clinging to the weapon, he brought it crashing to the floor, where he stood on its chest, defending against the second attacker. The one with the daggers leapt, and it looked down, seeing the weapon jutting through its midriff. He slid *Last One* out of its lifeless shell and brought it down upon Uhuria. It let out a single distorted whimper, then went silent.

The attack had lasted no more than two minutes. The crone hadn't moved. Rose advanced towards her, weapon gleaming with black oil.

Before he could reach her, the dragon arrived.

The monster was even more enormous than the pyre. It towered as tall as the dandelion trees in the Heartlands, with three sets of thin, spindly legs that stabbed into the ground. They joined its horrid, yellow flesh, as a long abdomen dangled beneath white, filmy wings. The head was uglier than the rest, with eight, black eyes, two twitching antennae, and a long, thin snout, if you could even call it that. On the end of it, jagged, cracked teeth buzzed at the pair of knights hungrily. Its circular jaw widened, and instead of a roar, a red glow began to flow down its throat.

Rose and Haera dove in opposite as the torrent of flame scorched the ground where they had been standing, leaving clouds of soot and smoke. Rose jammed his sword at one of the legs as it felt the ground, searching for him. It clanged off the slightly hairy skin, like steel against steel. The dragon leaned its head into the flames, shaking its leg annoyingly as the Rosewood Knight tried his move, and it sent him flying to the edge of the clearing. Dazed, his back against a tree that he had hit, he saw the creature inhale a portion of the flames, then immediately spit them out at Haera. She raised her shield over her head just as the heat met her, and Rose saw the wave of fire split around her.

Hands were grabbing him. The remaining marionettes had emerged from the shadows, and they were wrestling him into place as he attempted to break free. His sword and shield arm were pinned into place by the dozens of arms holding them there, reaching in from the shadows. They had not, however, held down his legs, as Rose soon discovered. Muscles crying, he slowly rose to one knee. His arms felt like they might snap from the strength of the mechanisms, but as he rose, they faltered, struggling to keep him in place.

Rose was standing on both feet, now, and he kicked back, sending one sprawling. That was all he needed. He slammed his sword and shield into the mass of wooden bodies, and soon they all fell to his blade, splinters and sawdust sent flying into the black forest beyond.

Haera was climbing one of the dragon's legs, gripping at the greasy hairs and pulling herself higher and higher. The beast was still sucking in the flames, belching and spraying it widely, drunk with heat. *Maybe she's onto something,* Rose thought. He strode over to where the crone was crying, tears spilling onto her face as the wind whipped her veil away.

"Ettiah," she muttered. "My Lady Moon's Blood. I have been your faithful servant, have I not? Will I see your dark reflection? The Abyss staring back? Oh, please do not make it so. Let me see your smile, my lady. Your smile."

The crone's eyes met his helm as he pointed his sword at her chin. "Why did you try to kill me?" He demanded. "A sacrifice for your pagan god?"

"Do you truly love her? The princess?"

"I will not have my honor as a knight questioned by a VVitch."

She looked behind him. "It seems Sir Haera does."

Haera had reached the dragon's back, and was digging her blade into its flesh, struggling to stay on as it reared and thrashed. Ichor was dripping down the dragon's sides.

The crone looked back at him. "Spoiled blood," she grinned, before jaws ripped into her stomach.

It was the dragon's mouth, its body leaning on the ground as it drank the blood from her body. In seconds, the crone had been drained, and she crumpled to the ground.

With a roar, Rose charged to the head of the creature and ripped open its flesh right between two of its eyes. Even as it gave one last, shuddering breath, he kept hacking, slashing, and stabbing, his anger blinded only by the blood of the creature splashing onto him. After the stench of the dead dragon hit him, he came to his senses and dug in his satchel, producing the feather. *Would Haera reach out and touch it? That would be an easy fix to my problem. Nay, if it is a duel she wants, it is a duel she will receive.*

This feather is already on its last of its so-called life. To use it on something other than the blood would be a waste.

Parting the flesh aside, he dug his hands into the steaming innards and lightly dabbed at the blood pooling amongst the meat and bones. Snapping off a piece of the now-calcified liquid, he stored it. He had not been precise with the feather, and so the creature was slowly petrifying. Haera kicked at the hard surface, testing it. She slid off the top of its back and back onto the ground, panting heavily.

"Thank you, Rosewood Knight."

He scowled, stepping away from the dead creature. He gripped one hand on his now-sheathed weapon. "Why?"

Her eyes traced to the place on his arm where she had cut him open, and she smiled. "Now I know that you can bleed." She grew solemn again. "Promise me one thing, before the duel. You will cure Lorenna. You were right. She deserves to be free."

Without a word, Rose nodded.

Haera began to walk briskly back into the treeline.

"Wait," the Rosewood Knight called.

She turned around.

"Why did you come here, if not to end me? Was this not our duel?"

Haera shook her head. "I do not think the gods would have recognized it, were Lady Lorenna not present. In any case, mayhaps I was craven. I ran from VVitch. I intended to run here, to let the dragon kill you, and so my problem would be gone forever." She continued walking. "That is not the way of the Midnight Sea. Waves do not cede before they hit the shore. The sand crumbles away before them, or they lap against the rocks, disappearing, and never to come back again."

With that, Lady Haera went off into the night.

CHAPTER THIRTEEN

Haera could not have been further from the sea.

Of all the names she had been given: Knight of the Roaring Dark, of the Midnight Sea, the Selkie, she just preferred Haera. Maybe, just maybe, after her duel with the Rosewood Knight, she would feel like she fit inside of her armor again. Forged in the heated fissures deep underneath the ocean, melted from a meteorite, and polished to perfection by her own two hands, it was Haera's pride and joy. It was not an inherited tool, though her sisters had offered her the pick of their family's legacy. It was not a forgotten relic from the Star Worlders. It was brash only in color. It was simple, and elegant in symbolism. Her armor, her sword, and shield were all Haera's.

No longer was she the one who had run from VVitch. *I am slayer of dragon,* and, Haera thought wryly, *lover of Lorenna.* Would her legacy be remembered as such, however? Would she be Haera Dragon Killer, Haera Lerelei? Or would she be Haera the Coward? Haera the Rose Slayer? Was she destined to live in the Rosewood Knight's shadow, just remembered as the one who abandoned him in his time of need, the one who stole away his bride-to-be?

The woods were not as frightening as they had been the night she ran from the VVitch. Instead of seeing strange, hooded figures in the dark, peering at her with white eyes, she only saw firebugs. They washed the forest in orange light, traveling in clouds so that they looked like ribbons of fire dancing around the trees, twirling and spiraling, leaving faint trails of light in their wake. Haera promised herself she would rest soon, but right now she was enjoying the journey back. At least she had these joyful creatures to keep her company. One landed on her nose, making her laugh as it tickled her with its pair of tiny, black antennas. Haera sighed, basking in the peaceful moment. She was lucky enough to have them. Lorenna, even now, was trapped in a cruel prison. Forced to be on the brink of freedom, only for the tower to snatch it away. Haera would reach her soon. *She had to.* There, with her princess as witness, she would put an end to the Rosewood Knight.

Always so headstrong, her sister's voice chided. *What will happen when the blood finally reaches up there, hmm*? Hestia tapped her knuckles against Haera's temple, as she always did, and Haera laughed, pushing her away. She was back in her palace under the sea. Her family were lined in front of the coral throne, the white-bearded King of the Midnight Sea regarding his daughters with an expression that might've passed for disapproval if not for that twinkle in his eye. Because of their customs, he rarely spoke a word, except when absolutely necessary. So it fell upon his eldest to hold court and rule the land as he bid her to. Hestia looked as all of them did, like Haera, except for her hair spilling onto the floor, braided and decorated with sea shells. She wore a beautiful orange and red gown, woven from the bioluminescence covering the coral reefs along the seafloor. What Haera loved best about her was even with her responsibilities, she still made time to laugh and clap along as her sisters danced to the music in the throne room.

Hestia sat on the left hand side of the king, on the steps leading to his chair. Directly to his right, standing rigid, trident in hand, was Hesperia. She wore black armor, polished so well that Haera could see her reflection perfectly along its surface. Her hair was cut short, even shorter than Father's. A red scar stretched from her neck to her cheek, but it only made her rare grins even brighter.

Some months ago, Haera had stood in the last place she usually found herself: the palace gardens. The palace itself resembled a small whale – one hundred and sixty meters in length, shaped in a fish-like oval that was mostly clear glass. Much like the night sky of the surface world, the black ocean brimmed with glowing life. Green jellyfish, enormous, pink squid, and schools made up of thousands of blue fish co-inhabited the wilderness around them, making for a stunning view outside every day. Inside, the palace was decorated with white columns and green curtains. Statues of ancestors past and guards in shining armor. *An Ettiah-like sculpture in the hull of an ancient Star leviathan,* as she had heard Father say once. Haera nor anyone else that she knew of could breathe underwater, as many popular myths liked to say, but she wished she could. Standing in the east wing, separated from the main royal halls, filled with exotic plants that could not have lived under the sea naturally, Haera looked out once more into the waters. Past the flora with a bright green stalk, its leaves tinged with red, which seemed to bleed onto the soil beneath, the droplets bouncing once, then splashing upon their second impact, watering the dirt.

"You're really going?" Hesperia leaned against the doorway, still dressed in her armor, though the trident was probably handed down to the next one entrusted to guard the king that night.

"Are you going to stop me?" Haera strode over, grappling her in a headlock, prepared to give her sister's head an appropriate amount of abuse. Hesperia twisted her arm back, pinning it behind her back. They locked eyes for a minute, then released each other, laughing.

"I don't think anything could stop you. That said, I know you know, but tell me you know again. Once you leave, that'll be it."

"I know."

"Have you told everyone?"

Haera nodded. "Hestia didn't take it well, but I think she understands."

"She's trying to make it harder for you to go."

Haera laughed again. This time it sounded hollow. "It's hard enough without my good sister's help." Hesperia hit her arm. "I mean that! But… thank you."

"What for?" Hesperia asked in surprise.

"For not taking it *too* badly."

Her expression shifted. For the first time in a while, she let Haera see the other side to her. Her vulnerable self. "Doesn't mean you won't be missed."

Haera embraced her, swallowing hard. "I know."

They walked arm in arm away from the garden. Haera took a look around her home, for what might be the last time.

"Diplomacy," Hesperia commented. "Politicking. What has become of the Haera I once knew?" She emerged from her bedroom, hair a tangled mess, dressed in her nightgown.

Haera and Hesperia shared a look, and Hesperia nodded, continuing her walk alone. There would be time for formal goodbyes in the morning. For now, Haera had business with her other sister.

"It's not really about that."

Hestia raised an eyebrow. "Will our ambassador not carry her kingdom's needs at beating heart?"

Haera rolled her eyes. "Of course I will, but I already explained to you, it's – my need, it goes beyond that. Don't you ever wonder what lies in the world above? Don't you ever wish to stare at the sky, through night and day? I wish that. I wish to feel the dry grasses, the ferocious wind in my hair."

"And understand thou the cost of such a change?"

She nodded, remembering the lines Hestia had forced her to memorize from their bylaws when they were younger. Haera had known the consequences of her decision when making it. "An ambassador from the royal family must never return, until her duty is complete. The attachments to her house must not cloud judgment of what might be best for diplomacy. Furthermore, I am not to be protected by the same laws a royal is entitled to. Any danger I encounter in the line of duty is to be purely mine own. The Midnight Sea does not shy from alliance, but it does not lust for it. An ambassador is sacred selfless."

Hestia nodded. "Finish thy duty quickly, sister."

That morning, Haera turned away from her family for the last time, for what would likely be a very, very long time. *Such is the cost of duty*, she told herself. *Such is the cost of freedom.* Haera stepped onto a square platform, and it began to rise from the floor. Where it had been, a deep hole loomed. The ceiling above her began to shift to the side, and when Haera reached her hand out, it met solid air. An invisible wall lay between her and the water cascading around her, to be swallowed into the pit. Her sisters' faces became distorted through the shield of air and water between them, and soon only the dark sea stared back.

She wore her armor and bore sword and shield. She would be gifted a steed by the watchtower on the mainland once she reached the surface. Haera hadn't felt this giddy since she was a little girl, opening a gift Father had given her. This was it. She felt an immense tug in her stomach as the platform rose faster. Years of training on statzel allowed her to maintain her balance. The ocean grew brighter, and the luminous aquatic life shrunk, turning into small pods and schools, swimming idly by as she rose above them all.

Just as Haera thought her blood would begin to bubble, the water rushed in around her, and she broke through the surface. Gray rocks jutted from the sand, spraying waves onto her. She shook her head, unsticking her hair from her face. The sun was impossibly bright. So impossibly beautiful. She dared not look it in its eyes, but she wanted nothing else but to. Haera had lived in darkness, surrounded by organic stars. Now she walked in daylight, splashed by black water. The air was cool and fresh. The sky exquisite like a violet.

Haera strode from the knee-height tide, startling a nearby marionette-manned fishing boat. The sea-side village was humble. A few wooden huts stacked on a cliffside overlooking the beach, with a stair, composed of planks precariously nailed into the rocks, the only path upwards. A marionette with a gray eyepatch over its eye and a rich, red cloak bowed to her at the foot. "Sir Haera. 'Tis an honor. I am Uhuria, servant to the Lord of the Willowood. She welcomes you to the land of soil and stone."

Haera gave a courteous head nod. "Please send her my thanks. Though this is not her domain, it is my understanding that she is gracious enough to send me on my way with supply?"

"Indeed. Your horse and belongings await you at the top. Please follow me."

A thin, tall keep sat upon an outcrop jutting into the ocean. The top held a balcony that circled its perimeter, with a room in the center containing a large, long-dead light. Crimson paint had faded away on its surface long ago. Tied to a post outside, was her horse. Bundles of food, water, and other necessities tied to the saddle.

"It's no statzel," apologized the marionette. "The Willowood is not the richest of kingdoms. This was all my Lord could muster."

"This is more than I could ask for," thanked Haera.

"My Lord hopes that you will visit her soon. Thou would be most welcome among our halls. If I may, my Lord also bid me I pass along a suggestion."

"You may."

"This land of which we stand on is the outskirts of the Heartlands. It is ruled by a royal family made strangers to the few who live in their kingdom. The princess resides in a tower not unlike this one, about four thousand kilometers away. You would do well to befriend her. Her land is trifled with plague and famine. She would be most grateful to anyone who aids her in her time of strife."

Up in the windows of the keep, a lone marionette watched Haera through partially closed curtains.

That night, as Haera continued her walk from the Willowood, she thought that was how she had earned the name of the Selkie. Those who put on the skin of a land dweller. The VVitch of children's bedtime stories, used by vengeful mothers. *Would I prove them true by becoming the monster they see in me should I defeat Rose? The destroyer of the idyllic knight and his princess? The foreigner who marched to their lands to claim what was not hers?*

The Rosewood Knight had cut down Uhuria. Haera had failed to save the lord of the Willowood. Had failed to even meet with her, as she had invited her to do. Haera had kept the invitation in mind as she had trailed Rose to the dragon, hoping to take shelter with the kindly old woman. Yet, he had beaten her to it, and even now, he held the future of Lorenna in his hands, instead of her.

Now she knew he could bleed. The Rosewood Knight was not the unstoppable warrior he and everyone else presented himself as. If this was the way the world worked – duels instead of dances, swords instead of words – then Haera would participate. She was not married to some romanticization of peace and harmony. Her knighthood had not come so easily. Hestia's jadedness had been hard won, just so as their mother's death had been hard lost. The Midnight Sea was united, at the death of all hundreds of soldiers from the Eldraerean Void.

Haera did not normally waste time wondering whether the gods would judge her for the blood on her hands. The sea would. It cared not for any living thing. It could choose to crush them like a grape, or soothe them like a lullaby. It was cold and warm, mysterious and comforting. It had looked upon her, and made her kneel, lifting Father's hand with Haera's sword to her shoulder. She had done what she had to in the name of duty, and her family was safe from invaders because of it.

A scream rang out from the forest. Deep, guttural. Haera had heard it before. Each time she swung her sword on the battlefield. She could almost see the soldiers watching her from the branches. Their pale expressions when she boarded their ship, armor stained and teeth bared, looked at her now, far away from the sea, yet still in the war.

The dark has a curious way of making you think, eh? Trepidation manifests like a weed choking bloom. A stifle to man's arrogance, because none of us are safe against which we cannot see. I did my duty, and now my kingdom is safe. I do not wish death upon my enemies. That wasn't quite true, though, was it? She did wish death upon them. They had come to her home. Her family, and she would defend it to the teeth. Should Selkie be born from vengeful love, so be it. Haera did not question her own actions.

Yet, she could still hear their screams. Mouths wide open. Why had the Rosewood Knight gone inside the madness? Was it truly just sheer, noble courage? Was Haera so pathetic a knight that she could not muster the strength to face the arbiter of ruin, devastator of her own devoted? This was why she had sworn to herself never again. She had come dangerously close to running away, while the Rosewood Knight was preoccupied by the marionettes. Yet, she had stood her ground. Stared into that helm of his, and showed him that she did not think him on par with some moon-faced god, as some did. She had seen him bleed tonight, and so she knew she could beat him. Slayer of VVitch he may be, but immortal he was not, as she had foolishly begun to wonder.

Haera fought the urge to draw her sword. The screams were in her head. A product of poorly-timed reflection. They were not there, despite her vivid auditory hallucination. Haera would walk the twilight after, not run from it. That was what she told herself, as she walked into the dark, awaiting what the new day would bring.

CHAPTER FOURTEEN

Morrel the marsh frog couldn't wait to go home.

He knew Mum would be cross with him. More than she had ever been before. He was afraid she wouldn't even look at him, as he knocked at their door. He wasn't even sure if Daeyvon and the others would want to keep playing games with him, not for a while, at least. Morrel had run away without saying goodbye. How could they forgive him for that? None of that mattered, though. It was enough just to be with them. Enough to be away from the cold mountaintop, and away from the thing which had looked like his friend.

Deborah was *fast*. They were already back on the familiar Heartland plains, red grass whirring past the streak of fur that the rabbit must've looked like to any passerby. He hoped Lorenna would understand when he came back to her empty-handed. Once Morrel went to see Mum, though, he *would* find a cure for her. He didn't know if VVitch had been telling the truth or not, when he said Morrel's heart would be what she needed, but VVitch told lies. All the bad people did, in Grandfather's stories. Even if his little frog heart was some magical ingredient, VVitch wouldn't have given it to Lorenna. He would've just used Morrel to do terrible things.

In a way, Morrel was glad he hadn't killed him. He wasn't sure what had taken the VVitch – maybe Starworlders, maybe something else. At least he hadn't had to take a life. Sometimes a knight had to, to protect everyone else, and he had been ready to, but he was thankful he hadn't been given the chance. That was not how he wanted to start his knighthood. Morrel wondered when Lorenna would make him a knight. After he found the cure she needed, probably, and that was alright. He wondered how her friend, the Rosewood Knight had become one.

Oftentimes he saw the Rosewood Knight arriving to Lorenna's tower on the other side of his grove, circling it, then leaving his horse and talking to the princess. True, she always giggled at his jokes and blushed at his lame compliments of the heart, but still, Morrel was not sure that he trusted the knight. For one, he had never seen him take off his helmet. Not once, and the frog saw almost *everything* that happened. Around the grove, at least. *A knight should have nothing to hide except his fear when slaying dragons.*

Now, here he was, all on his own, journeying across the Heartlands, scampering from grove to grove with many a song in his chest. He did miss his sword. His hands felt empty without it. However, a sword didn't make a knight. Their heart did, and that was something that perhaps even the greatest evil was right about.

Morrel left the rabbit far enough away from the grove so that the frogs wouldn't see it and get frightened. He knew it would never hurt them, but they didn't know that, and he didn't want to cause more commotion than he was already about to.

The grove looked exactly as he had left it, and he supposed it hadn't been that long. Birds and crickets chirped. Wind wove between the grass, and blew clumps of seeds off of the dandelion trees. The sun warmed his skin, and as Daeyvon, Cadissa, and Daniel broke through the trees, screaming and running toward him, he felt tears roll down his cheeks as he smiled. They tackled him to the ground, all laughing together.

"We missed you!" Cried Cadissa.

"Where've you been? What happened to your sheet?"

Morrel finally stood up, still grinning so wide he thought he'd tear his skin. Dae crossed his arms as usual, smirking at him.

"You came back."

"I did," replied Morrel. "I had to see Mum. I had to see Cadissa and Daniel, and…"

"And?" Asked Daeyvon.

"I had to see you. You're my best friend, Dae. Of course I had to see you."

Cadissa gasped. "Morrel, your mum! You have to see her!"

They pulled Morrel away. The grown-up frogs inside the grove all greeted him in surprise. Some with joy, others with a frown, but they all looked relieved. His friends led him into the familiar moss-carpeted tunnels. More frogs stared at him as he went. Then, he faced the hole in the wall that led to his home.

The others looked at him, as he looked at it. Dae nudged them. "C'mon. We'll let Morrel catch up."

When they were gone, Morrel walked inside.

Mum was hunched over a pot of stew. Her back was turned to him. She was just stirring, staring at the flames.

"Mum," Morrel said, his voice cracking.

Her hand stopped spinning the ladle. She didn't turn.

"I'm back," he kept going. "I– I came back, Momma. I saw the outside world, and it was beautiful and terrible, but I came back. I'm sorry, Mum. I'm sorry for running away. I'm sorry for not saying goodbye."

"Did you want to come back?" She asked, quietly.

He hesitated. "I felt awful for what I did. Both of us loved Grandfather, but I didn't want to put you through what he did again. I knew I had to come back, but…"

"But you only came back for me."

She turned around. She looked old and tired. She looked him up and down, and choked back a sob. Mum rushed toward him, wrapping him in a hug. "Morrel, my sweet, sweet boy. Welcome back."

They stood there for a long time, the two of them swaying back and forth, saying nothing. Then she stood back, inspecting him. "You look just like him, you know. Your grandfather would be so proud of you." She blinked back more tears.

"Mum? What's wrong?"

"I feel like… my little boy left in the night, and came back as a man today."

They both walked outside, hand-in-hand. Morrel said his proper hellos to all the other frogs, before being pulled away by his friends. They dipped their feet in the pond, laughing and catching up on what he had missed. Morrel didn't talk much about what had happened on his travels. They asked him, of course, but he brushed them off. Morrel and Dae shared a look, and he knew his friend understood. There wasn't anything to be said.

Mum joined them after a good bit of time. She wrapped him in a hug while they kept talking. Before, Morrel would've been embarrassed, but now, it just felt good to be in his mother's arms.

"You're going again?" Daeyvon asked in surprise.

Morrel looked at Mum. "I have a promise to keep."

She said nothing for a long time.

"Well, we'd better get you a fresh change of clothes, then. You look filthy."

They all helped him get ready this time. He changed into a fresh sheet, then put on Grandfather's armor over it. Dae, Cadissa, and Daniel all nervously approached Deborah, fastening a makeshift saddle, complete with all sorts of delicious snacks, plus a canteen of Mum's stew. Even though Lorenna's tower was right by them, Morrel wanted to ride the long way around the grove. To soak it all in, and appear presentable to the lady, instead of walking up to her all casual-like.

This time, saying goodbye was not so bad, because Morrel heard them all cheer for him as he rode away. Looking back, he saw Mum clutching his torn sheet, then let it blow away in the breeze.

Looking forward, he saw the moon in the sky, even though it was day. The land smelled like the end of summer. He tried to think exactly of how he could describe it. Like the rain, with endless plains of dry grass, and the earthy scent of freshly fallen leaves. It felt like something was coming to an end. Like the summer he had known before would never come again.

A rumble shook the planet.

From behind them, birds and rabbits took off, shooting past Deborah and Morrel. He hugged the rabbit's back, pressing his belly as tight as he could against the fur. The rumble grew louder, until the grass beside them parted to reveal two pairs of mechanical legs.

The Rosewood Knight rode past them, on his marionette statzel. He didn't see them – they were small compared to him, and the tall grass hid them well. He seemed intent on something. A trail of dust rose from behind him, and Morrel could see that he had come from the mountains. He had avoided the princess's tower entirely, and was heading in the direction of his home. When he had gone a little distance, Morrel urged Deborah to follow.

Once the rabbit saw the gray, ramshackle keep rising in the distance, it faltered, coming to a stop a good distance away. Its nose twitched, and its ear had peeled back. Morrel patted its head.

"It's okay if you're scared, Deborah. I'll be brave for the both of us. You stay back. I can go on ahead. It's always the knight who goes into the dragon's lair, and in the stories, the knight always walks back out." He slid off. "Stay put. I'll need a ride back home after this. Unless I take the Rosewood Knight's mount." He giggled. "Perhaps he doesn't deserve it." Morrel rubbed the rabbit's head once more. "No, no. I won't steal. Alright, I'll see you."

With that, he began to walk towards the castle. If you could even call it that. The bricks were moss ridden, crumbling. Parts of the structure had broken completely, and other parts had the naked, wooden frame exposed to the air. Clearly, this was an old ruin that had never finished being built. To Morrel's dismay, he did not see any roses anywhere in sight. *Is this not the Rosewood?* All that inhabited the space was places from eons past and a few, shriveled rose hedges.

He could see the knight dismounting, now. His dogs were barking from the kennel, a round building completely detached from the rest of the compound. Morrel saw Rose get a chunk of smoked meat from his bag, and throw it inside. The dogs barking turned to snarling, as the sounds of them fighting, tearing at the piece of flesh echoed all the way out there. Thankfully, Rose did not release them outside, and so Morrel crept closer, spying on the knight from a small bush, just outside the grounds of the keep.

He's going to go inside, then I won't be able to see him. Morrel circled the keep, placing himself in front of a window that overlooked the entrance hall inside of the building. As soon as he had taken his positioning just below the sill, he heard the Rosewood Knight knocking at the door. Morrel had never seen his face beneath his helm, but he imagined the knight's smile would be wide, stretched. Perhaps the flash of white teeth, but it would be discomforting for any person to look upon.

"Castellan!" Rose bellowed. He was not smiling, now. "Have you finally thrown yourself into the fire pit? Let me in! These are *my* halls. I will not be kept waiting like some dog begging for scraps. I've survived a basilisk, a dragon, and a crazed hag. I am very much looking forward to my chambers."

A dragon! Morrel thought, gleefully. Still, he kept peering into the window. The room was dark. A layer of dust covered the surfaces, as if it had not been kept for some time. A candle on the table inside was nearly gone, a stub of wax with a wick the only thing remaining from its former glory. He jumped as the door was smashed open.

"Damn you!" Rose roared. "When you come slinking out of your hidden corner, I'll give you a beating, I promise you that. Should you feel the need to do your part as my servant, I will be resting in my room." The knight's metal boots began thundering against the stone floor.

"My lord…?" Morrel heard a voice call out. Right in front of the window, the back of a marionette rose into view. It had been sitting just underneath, a mere inch away from where the frog now hid. "My lord… you've returned!"

His vision now covered by the Castellan, Morrel heard the Rosewood Knight stop walking. "Gods. What have you done to yourself?"

The marionette slowly began walking towards Rose. It had a gaited walk, half of its body slumping limp towards the floor. "I thought you were never coming back. I waited for you, oh, I did, but after the first four moons had come and gone, I grew certain you were not coming back. You were displeased with my work. Just like the last one. Oh, what a wretched thing I am. An old relic left behind by lords and ladies come and gone, from different times. A thing gathering dust in the corner, nothing but a nuisance for the Rose Knight. Still, we were content enough. At least, I had convinced myself. No, I see now. You could not wait to be rid of me. When you free Lorenna Lerelei from her tower – yes, I am certain that was the reason for your unexpected journey – you will leave forever, and once again I will be left alone."

The princess! Freed? Morrel's eyes had adjusted to the light. He could see Rose clearer now, who was backing towards the door. His posture seemed disgusted, as if backing away from a large, hairy insect. "This is not what I wanted."

The marionette laughed. "No? Have you not ridiculed my appearance ever since I came into your service? I was a bad servant, oh, yes, I was. I did not heed your command, but now you have returned, and I will be a *good* Castellan, now. Are you not pleased, my lord?" The marionette began grabbing the Rosewood Knight by the arm.

Morrel saw what the Castellan had done.

As far back as the frog could remember, marionettes had always shared one thing in common. They always had the white, crescent moon on one side of their face. Morrel quite liked it. They were always smiling a happy smile.

The Castellan had ripped the moon mask right off its face. The sunlight showed the gash that the action had carved into its features. Inside, bronze gears turned meekly, covered in cobwebs and constantly stuttering, as if removing the moon had caused some sort of damage. Wires and metal bits sparked bits of ember. Black oil ran dripped down its cheeks like tears.

Rose ripped his arm free. "Get away."

The marionette *snarled.* It drew a long, sharp kitchen knife and began slashing it at the Rosewood Knight. Rose dodged, and the knife carved off bits of wood from the door behind him. The marionette was howling, now, too, and Morrel's heart pounded. It was the scariest noise he had ever heard.

With one great thrust, Rose knocked the Castellan to the floor. It was still screaming when he drew his sword and split the marionette in two.

Morrel gasped and then realized his mistake. Before he could get away, the Rosewood Knight had grabbed him by the scruff of his neck and pulled him through the window. Morrel backed away against the wall, trembling, as the knight pointed his sword towards his face.

"What have we here? A child lost from home?"

Morrel closed his eyes. *For valor and Lady.* Willing himself not to falter, not to stutter, he rose to a standing position. The Rosewood Knight dwarfed him in size, but he did not care. He was not scared of someone who would kill their loyal servant out of disgust. As if squashing a bug. For the first time, Morrel saw this man for who he really was. "You have consorted with VVitch. I name you a liar, murderer, and traitor. In the name of the House of Lerelei, you will surrender, Rosewood Knight."

Rose stared at him a moment. His helm was removed. There was nothing between them but height, but that quickly changed as he kneeled. Morrel swallowed as his breath tickled his flesh. Then he began to laugh. A sick, barking laugh. "Run along back to your family, little frog. You are no knight, and I assure you, Lorenna will *never* make you one."

"I… I don't need to be a knight to do what's right."

Rose stood up. He appeared more interested now, his laugh gone. "Yes, I think you'll do." Before Morrel could react, he felt cold steel bite his belly, just below the heart. As his eyes began to close, he could make out Rose say: "Take solace, little one. You'll be serving your princess one last time."

CHAPTER FIFTEEN

The day of the duel had arrived, and the Rosewood Knight watched the final preparations.

A festival had made itself at home directly in the grass in front of Lorenna's tower. Great, white tents sprawled throughout the plain. Games with throwing darts, spinning wheels, and all manner of activity waited to be played. A dozen aurox had been slaughtered and prepared for the festivities. He watched as the butchers gutted them, pulling out their hearts and roasting them above spits for the fest goers to enjoy. His stomach rumbled as the smell of cooked meat hit him, combined with knotted fried bread slathered with honey, goblets overflowing with sweet wine, crackers dipped in melted cheeses, and even marionettes manning glass machines that spun edible pink cotton with metal, spider-like hands.

It had always been the Castellan who had made him meals. The pantries were full of spoiled food and sour bread. The livestock had died from starvation. Clearly, the Castellan had been neglecting his duties for almost the entirety of Rose's travels, and had cared for the dogs last, as they were alive and well when Rose arrived at his keep. Last night, he opted to nibble on a piece of stale bread, avoiding the areas green with mold. He soaked a washcloth over his face, then went to sleep. He did not dream very much anymore, but last night he had dreamt of the Castellan. His torn face screaming. It would all be worth it when he defeated Lady Haera in battle, and presented Lorenna with her cure. After that, she would love him until the seas went dry and the fire grew cold. He was sure of it.

To his annoyance, the duel that day would not be as simple as hand-to-hand combat. Lorenna had ordered the fair to come not only for her own amusement, but also at Haera's request. When he arrived at her tower, he found Haera already there, sitting on the railing of the balcony. *One fall and I win*, he found himself thinking. She did not even turn around when the Rosewood Knight spoke.

"My Lady of Lerelei! I have returned from my quest, and kneel before you today. For today is the day of my duel."

Lorenna smiled. "I am pleased to see you again, Rosewood Knight. Both of you. I am even more pleased that today is the day of your great duel. In the form of a tournament."

"A tourney, my lady?" Rose asked. Though his voice was steady, his thoughts were anything but. *A simple excuse for Haera to run from things again. She knows that death is forbidden in these things. That is why she urged Lorenna to turn it into a contest of lances and steeds.*

"Indeed, Rosewood Knight," Haera answered. "Unless you would prefer to submit now?"

He swallowed his anger. "I will make my preparations, Lady Haera. When we meet again, it shall be on the tourney field. May your god smile kindly upon you."

Rose turned away. What was there to do but obey the will of the princess of the Heartlands? The seats had already been arranged. A whole row of them at the base of her tower, her balcony of course being the spot of honor, and on the opposite end another row of seats. A temporary fence line had been built down the middle of the open strip of land in between. That was where Rose and Haera would face off, and that was fast, fast approaching.

They each had their own tent to make their preparations. Marionettes were milling about the fairground, either constructing the site of the tournament, or simply acting the part of a real, living thing. To avoid their blank stares, Rose stooped inside his tent. Lances had been laid out on a rack, all long and black, varying in length and weight. Picking up each one, Rose tested it, getting a feel for the one that would best fit his needs. Eventually, he settled on one twice the length of his arm. It was heavy, his arm growing tired after only a few minutes holding it, but it would do. His strategy in battle was brute force, and this would be no different. They were each allowed their own shield, one not necessarily assigned by the tournament. Rose had no idea what Haera's shield would be, but it would shatter underneath the force of his new weapon.

Another hour came and went. Rose paced idly in his tent, taking himself through sword drills, though according to Lorenna, they would not be needed. Still, he was nothing if not prepared. He jabbed and slashed at the training dummy that had been laid inside the tent. Gritting his teeth, he mutilated the thing, using all his strength to spill straw from its guts.

Breathing hard, he leaned on his sword, gazing at the wreckage left inside his tent. Haera's time was at an end.

When the time came, the horns bellowed deep, and Rose took one last swig from his flask. Leaving it in the tent, he strode outside. The sun gleamed off his newly polished armor. It had been scratched and burned throughout his journey, and so he begrudgingly let the marionettes fix it, standing as still as he could as they went over it with their shine and other such tools. He used the same shield as the night he and Haera had battled. The sigil of a thorned rose resided proudly on its front. It was forbidden for the tournament to provide new steeds, as they would likely not take to their new masters, and so he still mounted Windsoar, as Haera strode out of her tent on the other end of the yard.

The marionettes roared, their cheers and clapping reverberating off nothing. They stood and stomped, and Rose wished once again that their duel had been a private affair. After the proper amount of time, they fell silent in unison and sat back down.

Haera wore her green armor. It had been refurbished, as well, and it shone even brighter than his. She had taken her helmet off to greet the crowd, and despite the cuts and bruises on her face, she smiled, waving at the marionettes. A gust of wind passed by, tugging at her cape and hair, and Rose saw Lorenna blush. The two knights locked eyes, and Haera turned around, so that she was looking up at Lorenna. She gave the princess a deep bow.

"I will fight bravely for you, my love. I hope that you see that." Haera put on her helmet, and mounted her horse. It was not a marionette, nor even a statzel, Rose noted. *Even now, on her own playing field, I have the upper hand.*

On each side of the stands, trumpets at least three meters in length bellowed. A victorious laugh, welcoming the words of the Princess Lerelei. Banners swung from the necks of the trumpets, displaying her house sigil.

Lorenna clapped, and stood. A great, black crow perched upon her shoulder. Once again, the crowd cheered. Once they had quieted, she spoke: "It pleases me greatly for the fair to make such accommodations for me. I have always dreamed of seeing it, and now it is at my doorstep. 'Tis a marvelous day, indeed. Today, however, we are gathered to see the tournament of the ages. Two great knights wish for my hand, and one of them shall have it. The victor shall be my lord suitor. They shall be whom I love and call mine forevermore." Haera did not see, for her back was turned, but Lorenna's gaze seemed to flicker back to her.

No, Rose thought. *They are just your nerves*. He nearly laughed. *Nerves? What do I have to be nervous about?*

"Today, skill by lance and steed shall decide the winner," Lorenna continued. "The Rosewood Knight, slayer of VVitch and champion of the Heartlands, and Sir Haera, The Selkie, knight of the Roaring Dark, the Midnight Sea." She paused, and took a deep breath. "The first to score three points shall be victorious. I expect a fair battle, and both of you... be careful." Lorenna cleared her throat, then clapped her hands together. "May E– may Ahmer look favorably upon you." Just like that, the battle had begun.

Rose spurred his steed into motion. In his left hand, he held his shield, and his right, the lance. He was descending upon the Selkie like a crashing wave. Windsoar's wings were in full motion, propelling it faster as it galloped across the ground. Haera grew closer, and he pointed his shield to hers outstretched. It was the same as the night of the dragon. *The kraken will drown today.*

The lance clapped the shield as it struck, sliding off the smooth metal as the tip left a long, white scrape against the surface. The impact had not been terrible, and so he finished riding the length of the field, unshaken, turning and switching sides as Haera did the same on the opposite end.

"I thought the dragon slayer was with us today!" Haera called out, and the crowd jeered. Rose felt the anger begin to rise to his head, then promptly extinguished it. *I will not allow her to play such games with me.*

Cooly, he replied: "The dog barks at her master's heels. Tell me, will enough tricks convince your Lady Lerelei to love you?"

Immediately, Haera charged again. Her horse was clad in matching green armor, with black trim. It covered its head and body, though its legs had to be left bare so that it could run. This time, Rose tried to slam his lance down on top of her shield, in an attempt at knocking it from her grip, and possibly breaking her arm in the process. It seemed she had anticipated his move, and in response, shot the shield up when he came upon her with his lance. The force of the impact sent the weapon spinning into the air, eventually embedding itself into the ground. The crowd clapped. Haera had scored the first point. Lorenna was cheering the loudest, laughing and clapping her hands. *Is this just a game to her? Does she not realize what is at stake?*

They took a short break to get readjusted. Marionettes fetched Rose a new lance. He saw Haera chatting with Lorenna, both of them laughing at some jape too far away to hear. *Even between strikes, she flirts, making even the smallest move to win Lorenna's heart.*

Then a marionette standing on a wooden tower just beyond the stands blew the instrument, signaling the second round. Rose wished the tournament was between the thing and him, so he could end the puppet's incessant noises. He mounted his marionette. Windsoar ran. *Ignore the shield. Aim for her smug face.* As the pounding of hooves washed all other noises out, he studied her stance atop the saddle. She held her shoulders straight, lance at a perfect angle, shield up. It seemed the knight had finally found her backbone. Rose could not wait to break it.

He saw the gleaming armor grow closer. It was that, and the purple sky around. The sky, with the moon glaring down upon him. The Rosewood Knight felt steel clash against steel, then the hooves were drowned by a marionette's screams.

In his distraction, he had failed to notice Haera pointing her lance not for himself or his shield, but for one of Windsoar's fluttering wings. Upon impact, the metal weapon had ripped through the thin material, tearing at the wooden membranes and muscles that had allowed the creature to fly. Now, black oil spilled from the tear, wind moving through it and fluttering the material. The horse finished its run, then stopped, neighing wildly. Rose attempted to calm it. He saw Haera turning around for another go. *Damn her.*

He spurred Windsoar, despite its resistance. *C'mon. We'll dismount her and win this thing. I'll fix your broken wing. Just get me through this.* His fury was apparently enough, as the force dug a hole through her shield and hit her square in the chest, knocking her off her horse.

"One point to the Rosewood Knight," Lorenna called.

As they took positions again, Rose saw Haera shrugging her shoulders, stretching the no-doubt tired muscles. She had apparently run out of taunts as she had met this first loss of point.

You broke my horse, so I'll break yours.

They thundered towards each other, the hole in Haera's shield blatantly obvious. She had insisted on keeping it, and so now she looked significantly more battered than before. Rose leaned forward, and speared his lance through the unprotected calf of her horse's leg. Haera flew forward, hitting the ground with a thud that undoubtedly tremored her oceanland itself, and rolled forward. Her howl would be enough to topple mountains.

"Point to the Rose," Lorenna said grimly. The marionettes were cheering for *him*, now. They cheered louder still when Haera rose quickly to her feet. She wiped blood off her nose.

Shink. Haera drew her sword, throwing her broken shield to the grass. "Rosewood Knight, I demand a trial by combat." She waited, letting the words hang upon the noose. Then she released the gallows. "To the death."

"NO!" Lorenna screamed, throwing herself from the balcony. The crow flew off her shoulder, watching as she tried to reach Haera. The vines covering the tower immediately grappled her, leaving her arms restrained as she struggled fruitlessly. "Haera! Don't do this! I tried to help you. Don't you see?! I tried to help! I love you, oh, I love you, I love you!"

Haera lifted her helmet and gave the Lady Lerelei a smile. "I will win this for *us*, Lorenna."

Irritated, Rose spoke: "I accept your challenge." He dismounted and drew *Last One*. He cast his own shield aside, as well. By all the laws of gods and men, this would be a fair fight. It had to be.

Haera put on her visor. She squared her stance, holding her longsword in both hands. She was ready. She hoped.

Immediately, he strode forward, and brought his burning sword down upon her, pressing her blade closer to her protected face as his strength pushed the blocked weapon back. *Lorenna loves ME. What nerve does this knight have, coming here from a queer land, and stealing the princess away with the tug of a smile?* "Haera is CRAVEN!" He roared up at Lorenna, as she watched them battle, hands covering her mouth in fear. The Selkie was parrying every thrust, blocking every slice. "Do you see now, even in her own challenge, how she does not fight back?!" In a quick motion, he swung at her legs. She side-stepped, waltzing back around him. He raged. "Is this the woman you wish to wed? One too cowardly to fight?"

Lorenna had tears running down her face. They were blue; they twinkled magnificently, not making a single imprint on the white balcony as they spilled. As Haera side-stepped, she spun around and whirled the blade at Rose's unprotected back. It clanged off him, the impact forcing him to jolt forward. The momentum was making him fall to the ground. As he realized this, he switched so that he was twisted towards Haera, and blocked her strike just as he fell into the dirt.

She was upon him, battering his steel blade with a whirlwind-like force. He had only one hand free as he used the other to shuffle himself away, hoping to gain a moment to get back up onto his feet. She seemed to know what he was doing, and would not allow it. With every strike of her blade, he was given perhaps half a second before the next one came, sending his arm slightly lower and lower to the ground as its muscles struggled to keep up with the weight of the sword and the battering attacks.

Enough of this. Upon the next swing from Haera, he curved his own sword through the air, smashing it against the side of her blade and causing it to briefly point towards the ground. The Rosewood Knight took the opportunity to grip Haera's shoulders with both hands and use the momentum to hoist himself to his feet. Before she could react, he slammed his helmet into her own.

Haera stumbled back, her head tilting to one side, looking dazed. Rose brought his sword down upon her shoulder. The metal there was not enough to prevent the crack of her bones on impact. She yelled, clutching her arm. He had not hit her sword arm, but she was still without a functioning one, and he was back on his feet. Their blades met yet again, dancing in a ringing battle of flashing sunlight and scraping steel. Before long, Haera had resorted to kicking dust into the air in front of her in the patches of ground where the grass had not yet grown.

The clouds of dust did not help, however. Rose was advancing, now meeting all her attacks with parries and blocks of his own. As he lifted his blade for another attack, Haera performed a high kick, bringing the heel of her boot down on the flat end of the sword, briefly pinning it to the ground as she now stood on it. As Rose used both of hands to begin prying it from beneath Haera, she shoved her blade in the gap between his breastplate and his shoulder plate. It went clean through, turning red as the blade tasted the air on the other end. She slid it out. As he moved his arm out of the way, the end of her sword caught the tip of his ring finger, severing it.

He howled, curling his bloodied hand as a final surge of adrenaline kicked in. He swept *Last One* from beneath her foot, and arched it so that it met her helmet, sending it flying off her head. Rose grabbed her longsword in his hand, curling his bleeding fist once more, so tight that he felt the steel snapping beneath his armored palms. Haera's smiling face beamed up at him and he began to beat it.

She spat out blood as she laughed. "At–"

He hit her.

"Least–"

He hit her again. Rose paused, lungs burning with exhaustion.

"I got one good hit in." Haera turned to look at Lorenna, still tangled in the vines. "I'm sorry I couldn't come back this time."

Rose looked down. In his fury, he had noticed Haera slide her sword into his ribcage. He looked at her again. She was not looking at him.

Rose spat in her swollen, pulpitulated face. He did not hear Lorenna's screams as he brought his sword down on Haera's head. Her blood sprayed onto her shield, left abandoned on the ground. For one brief moment, the Rosewood Knight could have sworn that a sound filled his ears, before it was gone in an instant. The sound of waves crashing against a shore.

CHAPTER SIXTEEN

Lorenna Lerelei looked vacantly at the gray sky.

It had been a week since Haera had died. Sun-Bright had not once peeked through the canvas of dark gloom that covered the Heartlands. In her wardrobe, she had found equally as black clothing presented for her. The day of Haera's funeral, Lorenna had donned a dark gown, the collars and bindings choking her wrists, chest, and neck. Her antlers were obscured by a hood attached to the clothing, edged with gold. It felt cold as the heat of the day made the dress stick to her.

Haera's sisters had received word, and came in a stampede of horses and sorrow. They all wore hoods of shimmering orange and yellow. Beautifully crafted, silk-like material that resembled flames. The fire crowded around the casket, blessing their fallen sibling. She expected them to curse Lorenna's name, to point crossbows at her and declare a forever war against the Heartlands. Instead, the oldest of her sisters looked up at her.

There were so many things she could have said, so why had those words come out of her mouth? "Did you love her, Lady Lerelei? Haera loved you. She died for you."

Lorenna watched from her balcony: Haera's coffin lifted by a procession of marionettes and humans alike. They gripped the rich wood, the top wood-burned with the sigil of the rising kraken. Lorenna stared as it grew farther and farther away, the procession making its way towards the Midnight Sea.

The moon was visible that day, as clouds parted to reveal its cracked face. "Be good to her," Lorenna had whispered.

The sisters had stacked, smooth, gray stones on top of each other. They were balanced perfectly, so that they teetered on the edge of falling, but not even the wind could move them. The cairn lay in the grass beneath Lorenna's balcony, and it seemed as if Haera was reaching for her. Outstretching her hand one last time.

Today, Lorenna lay in her bed. She gazed up at the sky, then to the ceiling, the one she had gazed up at so many times. A new crack had formed. Thirty-two now. *If this tower of mine crumbles, will I be forced to lay crushed amongst the ruins?* She half expected a flake of the roof to flutter down and land on her nose in response, but instead, she kept staring, and the ceiling stared back.

"Oh, Haera. How tortuous it is to be trapped between two worlds, so. Mine was of two knights, competing for my hand. You proved yourself a worthy champion, indeed." Tears threatened to well up again. "You just had to prove yourself courageous in the end, didn't you? Haera, why? Didn't you know? I always knew how brave you were. I always knew how valiant your spirit was, and eventually, I found I always knew that I loved you."

The vines rustled outside. There was no wind. Slowly, Lorenna sat up. She felt no fear. Rather, irritation. *Will you not allow me time to grieve, Mater?* Still in her funeral gown, she stormed out of bed. Her bare feet padded against the floor, growing faster as her fury rose. She grabbed a hold of one of the vines, ripping it from its stem and throwing it away from the tower. The green mass kept twirling and moving, avoiding her best attempts at fighting it. Finally, the Lady of Lerelei howled, tearing the white petals away in a rain of fluttering white, and sat on the floor, cradling her head in her arms, and crying.

"Why could I not do more for you, Haera? I sh– I should have done more. I should've, I should've, I should've! You gave me my taste of freedom, and I squandered it! Mother was right for keeping me here. I hurt those around me. You would have been better off not knowing me. It may as well have been me holding the blade."

Something clattered against the marble floor in front of her. Sniffling, she unstuck her head from her arms, wiping away tears as she looked at the thing that had been presented before her. It was a golden goblet, gripped by the very vines that she had been ripping away moments before. The cup was inlaid with red gemstones, nearly touching the brim. Inside, a deep red liquid stood still. It smelled sweet, like wine.

Carefully picking it up, she stood up, edging closer to the railing. Cupping it in the palms of her hands, it felt warm beneath her touch. Looking down, she saw the Rosewood Knight kneeling. He had his sword placed in the ground, his gauntlets resting on its hilt. Lorenna noted the finger that was missing, the armor torn from the rest of the glove by Haera's strike with her blade. His breathing was laborious. Clearly, the duel had taken more out of him than he cared to admit. Slowly, he raised his helm to look at Lorenna. Gooseflesh ran down her arms.

Before she could speak, Rose's voice cut through the air. "My Lady of Lerelei. I ask that you do not speak. I know already of the words you have chosen for me. I have no right to request an action from you, yet I have one. A monumental one, that shall change your life and mine forever. It is a simple one, yet not at all." He stood up, taking his sword and sheathing it. "Lady Haera had but one last request of me. One I intend to honor. Lorenna, please drink from the cup."

Lorenna looked down at the cup. She then realized that it was not wine at all.

Haera, the first place I shall walk to is the Midnight Sea. Taking a deep breath, Lorenna closed her eyes as she drank from the goblet. It was icy, oozing down her throat, much like mucus brought on by a cold. She exhaled, feeling it pool into her stomach. On her tongue, it tasted like the most bitter, sour, sweet thing she had ever had. Tears ran down her cheeks as she opened her eyes once more.

Slowly, Lorenna placed her foot on the railing. She gripped it with her hand, and raised her entire body to rest on its edge. The vines began to curl around her, though they felt looser. Less restricting. She was sitting on the edge, now, and with one simple push, she leapt off the tower. The fall turned into a glide, as the vines kept her from plummeting, and she stretched just one finger towards her knight, and he returned the gesture. She was laughing. Rose grabbed a hold of her hand and caught her before she could hit the ground. The vines were gone. Lorenna looked up at him, cradled in his arms.

"Are you to be my lord husband?"

He nodded. "And you, my lady wife. Any beasts, any VVitch, that threaten these lands, will be yours to rule, and mine to slay should they insult your perfect beauty." He lowered her to a standing position.

Feeling an inexplicable rush of happiness, Lorenna grabbed him by his arms and they spun in a circle. *She was free!* "How delicious the autumn air tastes!" She exclaimed. "Summer has fallen, but *oh*, how the air thrives!

The grass is so soft." As they danced, Lorenna ran a hand along the outer surface of the tower. "The bricks are so warm!" She turned, closing her eyes, and basking in the midday sun. The clouds had parted, allowing beams of light to cover her bodice.

The Rosewood Knight ran his hand along her cheek. The metal was cold to the touch, yet Lorenna placed her own hand over it. He smelled like a garden of roses. Sweeter than the very flowers that grew beneath her feet. She felt his gauntlet. The greaves and ridges of the fine craftsmanship. She felt each finger. The thumb, the index, the middle, and…

Lorenna pulled away, feeling a headache pierce her thoughts. *No, no, no, no…* "I smell VVitch." She looked at the Rosewood Knight.

His shoulders tensed. They were strange. Hunched. "'Tis the smell of the flowers, my lady. You have not yet grown accustomed to them."

Rose's armor had been quite battered. Scratches ran along its surface. The fabric beneath was stained red. Faint scorch marks had been attempted to be scrubbed away. The sword in his sheath was caked in dirt from the ground. "My lady wife –"

Lorenna's eyes widened. A shadow crossed over the land. Deep, black clouds. She looked at the empty goblet, lying on the ground. Remnants of the liquid were trickling out. "What did you…? What did you put in that?"

He wrung his hands, backing away. His steed stood tall in the background. "Only a potion to rid you of your curse. I swear –"

Lorenna could no longer feel the grass beneath her feet. "Swear by whom? Ettiah? The goddess you scoff at when anyone mentions her name? The one who you curse in secret? Or do you swear by *your* gods? What even might they be? You have never, not once, told me where the Rosewood is. I know not what gods you worship, what laws you follow. Only the ones you invoked to challenge Haera to a duel."

The veil had been blown off her head. Her hair was waving in the air. She realized that she could not feel the grass because the grass was no longer beneath her feet. Lorenna levitated, rising in front of the Rosewood Knight as he cowered before her. The wind was howling with the pain of a loved one that had been lost. Thunder boomed, rain pouring down in a fierce shower. Hail pelted Rose, pinging off his armor as he raised his hands to shield himself. The missing finger tasted the dew-sweet air.

"She brought that upon herself," He snapped. "She *stole* your honor. Haera stole it away, and who here chose to defend it?"

A bolt of lightning flashed, striking a tree nearby. The flames roared to life. Rose winced. Though the heat was several meters away, he seemed to feel the fire as if it was inches away from his flesh.

"It is you who is without honor, Rose. Tell me true, is it I whom you crave, or my kingdom? Would you treat me as your wife, or your pet? Kept tightly leashed, so that you may set me loose on any who dare question your word. Look at me ascend upon you, now. Do you even comprehend what I am? Do you know that I am more than just some mere princess for you to steal away?"

The Rosewood Knight turned and ran. His cloak caught between his legs, and he paused to untangle it. Lorenna felt her fury blossom, and she descended upon him as he reached the saddle of his horse. They grappled, Rose panting as he used his overwhelming strength to pin her to the ground. He was reaching for something in his satchel. Screaming, Lorenna's eyes shone bright as she threw him away from her, shoving him as he unclasped the cork from his flask. He was groaning in pain and misery, clutching his sides with one hand as he used the other, flask between his fingers, to wrench the helm from his head.

The Rosewood Knight was rotting. Melting skin dripped from his face in clumps, sickly green in some places. Worms were crawling inside one of his empty eye sockets. His lips had fallen off, leaving only bleeding, saggy flesh between his yellow teeth and his jaw as they tasted the flask he held up. He gasped as nothing came out of the bottle. His head was bald, hair long fallen off the mottled, puss-infested skull. Scars ran across his cheeks, some thorns still embedded just beneath the surface of the skin. His one eye met hers, red veins webbing over its white, glossy material.

"You will be my wife! Everything I have done, it is for the good of the kingdom! I would be your lord husband. You shall be my lady wife," Rose cried, covering his face as the rain dripped off the place where his nose had used to be. He was rasping. The rattle was the most disgusting sound Lorenna had ever heard. He reached up towards her.

"Get away," Lorenna said. From her fingertips, brown vines sprouted, running onto the ground, enveloping the knight.

They twisted around him, growing thicker and stronger. It was covering his sword, his armor, his chest. His limbs reached towards the sky, then immediately retracted. Lorenna looked and saw that the moon was visible once more. Rose said something muffled before the bark closed around his head.

The plant kept growing. It was getting taller, branches sprouting from its trunk. Frosty blue buds began to bloom, opening. Opening until they were revealed to Lorenna, and a canopy of ocean stood before her. She went back down onto the ground, walking towards the tree. She plucked a blue rose from its branches.

EPILOGUE

Lorenna Lerelei, princess of the Heartlands, heard a voice call out to her from behind.

She had never heard the voice in memory, but missed it all the same. It was the voice of a shadow just outside her peripheral vision that she so often saw in her room. The one that provided but never was. Lorenna knew it was the voice of her mother.

"My *Ahmer.*"

Crying, Lorenna turned around. A woman stood before her. Over three meters in height, long, curly red hair hung off her head. Half of it was obscured by a white, smiling mask. The other half was flesh of sky and stars, twinkling and shining. She wore a white robe, going all the way past her feet and dragging on the crimson grass. In one hand, she studied the helmet of the Rosewood Knight.

Ettiah and Ahmer, the Moon's Blood and her Sun-Bright Child, began to talk.

The sun spoke first. "Mater. You're here."

"Yes, I am, Ahmer. I am here."

"Why?"

The moon paused. "Why?"

"Why do you come now?"

"I come when my child needs me the most."

"Your child needed you when she grew up alone, in an empty tower. When she went to bed weeping every single night, wishing her mother would come. Still, she needed you, when great time had passed, and she began to say she hoped she would never see her mater again. When she… when *I* thought I had found true love, and when I truly did, and then when it was ripped away from me. I needed you, and you saw, and you did not come."

The moon let the helmet fall to the ground. The armor was a curious little trinket, as well as the sword, but her interest in it had passed. "You are beginning to learn what you are truly capable of, Ahmer. I can only interfere so much. The whims of man are a trifle thing. It is a hard lesson to learn."

The sun thundered, "Must it be a lesson at all? We are not what they call us, truly. Yes, I am beginning to remember. We are beings that they call gods. We are Ettiah and Ahmer or whatever name they have thought up. Did Haera learn the hard rules of man? Was her demise an Abyssal jest?"

The moon's face frowned. Stars moved, replaced by black, cosmic void. They formed a ring around her body, spinning faster and faster. A wave of shadow seemed to spill from her head of red hair, darkening the sky until it eclipsed the sun. The moon grew and grew, even taller than before. The ring of stars broke. Her voice was changed. Deepened and said in the dialects of a thousand tongues. "You wish to learn the thoughts of death? Challenge the way things have been since Ettiah shattered birthing you? Very well, Ahmer, I shall tell you. Look upon the true face of Abyss. That which is furthest from the moon and sun's light. Ettiah nor I had any wish to see the Selkie die, nor Morrel. Yes, the frog perished at the hands of the Rosewood Knight. To break your curse, Ahmer. The creature died for *you*, and such is the way of so-called gods. We are above the transgressions of man, yes, but must beware their love. Abyss, Moon's Blood, and Sun-Bright shall stand until the end of eternity and witness all love die at our feet. Witness men be born and find their purpose and find love and then die, and this cycle you are a witness to, Ahmer. The sun grows too big, so you will be made humble and sent into mortal form to look upon the sins of man. You are their champion, and so no, you will not be with Ettiah. You will be down here with them, in forms that their minds can comprehend. She will be forced only to look upon you at night, and you will be here. You bring joy and witness death. You are life."

Cicadas buzzed. Birds sang. The sun swallowed. "But I love. I cry."

The shadow faded. The moon had returned, and she could think of nothing to say. She beckoned for the sun to follow her. They tread across the Heartlands. Gazed upon a family of rabbits, nestling together in their burrow. Heard the dirge of the marsh frogs from within the groves, witnessed young pups free from their cages, playing together in the grasses. Smelled the smoke from wildfires far, far away.

The sun stood in a creek, long since dried, and felt water flowing there once more, washing her feet of dirt and grime. She followed it all the way to the sea, green grass growing in her wake, and stood in the dark waters. The salt tinged the air.

"Do you know what day it is?" The moon asked.

"The first of Autumn," the sun replied. "You'll be leaving again. I won't see you for a long time."

"You can change form, if you wish. I cannot promise that you will not learn these lessons again. New forms bring new memories, though parts of you shall remain. I will not, however, make you stay in your tower. I… that was wrong of me. Do you wish to be someone else? Live your life through different eyes?"

The sun took a long time to answer.

ACKNOWLEDGEMENTS

I can't believe *For Sword and Planet* is actually out. I first have to thank my family for supporting me as I worked tirelessly to write this book. Thank you, Leaf, Rain, and Juniper. Thanks, Papá, for being a writer yourself and inspiring me through your works of poetry and prose. Thanks, Mom, for being the hardest worker I know. Thank you Uncle Mike, Paul, and Aunt Steph, for always believing in me. Thank you, Uncle Andy, for being the strongest human on any planet.

Next, I'd be remiss to not thank all my friends who have been priceless throughout my long writing process. I'd like to thank the *D&D* group: Ezan, Gael, Meleena, Isla, Cynthia, Qeter, and Seren, for being the inspiration behind my characters. Thank you, Ella, for creating the wonderful cover and pieces of art for *For Sword and Planet.*

I'd like to thank my friend and editor Joe, for being the connection I needed to get my novel seen. Thank you, Robbie and Andy at Shy City House, for tirelessly editing and polishing this novel to its fullest potential.

Lastly, thank you, reader, for taking the time to peruse my really weird book. I hope that, if anything, I can demonstrate that anyone can be published, and follow their crazy ideas. I hope it wasn't too hard trying to pronounce "VVitch."

Milton Keynes UK
Ingram Content Group UK Ltd.
UKHW022249280824
447491UK00011B/428

9 798330 359660